1

I first saw Sarah from the window of a train — a train taking me to a house where I was not welcome.

I had been in a nearly fatal airplane crash and now I was coming to visit the mother who had abandoned me years ago. I no longer thought of her as my mother. She was just a woman I didn't know and hadn't seen in almost twenty years.

But there was something about the brightness of the early morning sun that did wonders for my low spirits. Even the food tasted better and the plaster cast on my leg felt less weighty.

The waiter put my check discreetly at the edge of the table and refilled my cup.

'We'll be arriving at Gulf Point in about five minutes, Miss Whelan,' he said.

I smiled. 'Thank you. I'm all ready.'

He bowed slightly and left me to my thoughts.

The dining car was practically deserted. Not very many people came to this part of Florida at this time of year. I'd been warned that it would be hot and muggy and swarming with insects. That didn't bother me half as much as the thought of having to live under the same roof with *her* — the great Diana Hamilton of stage, screen, radio and television.

Who would, of course, prefer to forget the radio part of that. It was her obsession with staying young that had meant keeping my existence a secret. Diana Hamilton couldn't afford to have a grown daughter. Her public might lose interest, especially her young public.

'There is a very obvious generation gap, and rightfully so,' she had said in a teenage fan magazine interview. 'And the young among us want to be free of the old ways and old ideas . . . '

I shook my head. She had to be fifty at least, but she deceived herself so much that I think she actually believed herself to be a young maiden.

Daddy used to tell me about her — how beautiful she was, how talented, how impossible to live with. He likened her to a little girl who refused to grow up. She couldn't accept the fact that she was aging.

When I was three, she abandoned us. At nine I found myself an orphan and it was then that I'd had my last contact with her, of an indirect sort — a letter from a law firm informing me that I would be amply provided for financially. I was to be placed under the supervision of guardians and it was made plain enough that Diana Hamilton wanted no further association with me.

The woman across the aisle rattled her newspaper and began to eye me. I could tell by her look exactly which page of her paper she was reading. My picture was on that inside page, and the picture of Diana Hamilton was next to mine. And I knew the caption well. I'd seen it often enough of late. It read: 'Long lost daughter of actress lone survivor of plane crash.'

When I chanced a glance toward my dining companion, she looked at me over the edge of the paper and gave a faint smile. I looked away immediately in order to discourage any conversation. Everyone who recognized me said the same things. 'Wasn't it lucky for you that they found out your true identity? You must be so happy.'

I wasn't happy — I'd always known my identity — and I wasn't a long lost daughter. I wanted to tell them all just how the great Diana Hamilton really had abandoned me, refused to recognize me as her own flesh and blood, because a grown daughter might tarnish her youthful image. She didn't want me now any more than she ever had. She'd been forced to accept me when fingerprints taken while I was unconscious had identified me. My birth certificate came to light. Sharp reporters were quick to put names together.

It was only then that the talented Diana played her most dramatic scene. Her poor, dear lost daughter, she had told the reporters. Her first husband had disappeared, taking their little child with him. She didn't want a scandal. She searched as thoroughly as she dared, but then her studio sent her to Europe on location and her search had to be interrupted. Eventually that search was tearfully abandoned when Phil Whelan's trail grew too faint and too cold to follow.

I suddenly smiled to myself. I could see her ranting and raving behind closed doors. She was forced to send for me. Her public demanded that . . . and I knew it infuriated her.

Why hadn't I spoken up and given my account of the true story to the newspapers? I hadn't, I only sat and kept quiet. What would it have accomplished, after all, to ruin Diana Hamilton's image? So, yes I had gone along with her charade, with this reunion put on for the benefit of the press and her public.

The woman across the aisle rattled her paper again, trying to catch my attention. I quickly finished my coffee, left money on the table, and hurried out of the dining car on my crutch, being careful not to look in the woman's direction.

I heard her mumble an 'Excuse me, Miss Whelan,' when I passed her table, but I pretended not to hear. I made my way back to my compartment, determined to hold my low spirits at bay. I could get through this well enough, and in no time at all I'd be back in Hillsborough, teaching school. Diana would tire of playing the part of the happy, munificent mother within a week and I'd be free to go back to the life I knew.

The conductor tapped on my door. 'We're coming into Gulf Point, Miss Whelan.'

'Thank you.' I began stacking my suitcases on the seat.

It was at that moment that I saw Sarah Braddock. The train was slowing, its bell clanging as we started toward the station. I saw a girl running across a field just outside my window, running as though the devil himself were chasing her. And the man pursuing her might well have been the devil by the look of him in his black chauffeur's uniform, the visor of his cap flashing in the sunlight like flames from Satan's fires.

He overtook her and grabbed hold of the girl. She fought to get free of him. I might have passed the whole incident off as merely some wayward, wealthy young lady who was rebelling against her established family, or her chauffeur, for some capricious reason, but he struck her.

I stiffened with revulsion. She went limp and he scooped her up into his arms and carried her toward a long, sleek car which I hadn't noticed before, an old-fashioned limousine from the forties.

Just then the door to my compartment opened and the porter came in. He started to collect my baggage.

'Quick,' I said, pointing out the window. 'A girl is being abducted.'

The porter merely stared at me.

'Look. There in the field.'

Unfortunately, the train was still in motion. First a line of trees obscured the view, then a billboard, then more trees. Before I realized it the train was clanging to a halt alongside the station.

I completely forget about Diana Hamilton, my broken leg, my luggage, my supposed recuperation. I grabbed up my crutch and hobbled quickly past the porter and started off the train. I didn't give a thought about anything except that poor unfortunate girl. I had to do something. I couldn't just let her be dumped into a limousine and spirited away to heaven knows what fate. Perhaps if I acted quickly enough, the authorities might overtake the limousine and confront the driver before he had a chance to get the girl too far away.

I hobbled down the length of the passageway, down the metal stairs of the coach.

'Watch your step, Miss,' the conductor said when I almost tripped and fell. He grabbed my arm.

'I just saw what I think was an abduction,' I said breathlessly. 'Where is the station master's office?'

He just looked at me rather blankly. 'Beg pardon?'

'Which way to the station master's office? A man is abducting a young girl. I saw them from my window.'

'But . . . '

And then they descended upon me.

'Darling,' Diana Hamilton called, advancing toward me with her entourage of newspaper men, photographers, well-wishers.

My heart sank. 'Oh, no,' I moaned and turned a pleading eye to the conductor. 'I saw a girl knocked unconscious and put into a limousine. You must do something.'

He gave me a suspicious look, a faint smile and then eased by me and got back up on the steps of the train.

Seconds later I found myself completely surrounded. I looked for help, but it was useless. I was trapped.

'Darling,' Diana said again, her voice high and affected. I could barely make out the exaggerated smile behind the heavy veil she wore. She hugged me to her and I cringed inwardly. 'Alice. How simply marvelous to have found you at last.' She turned me — forcefully — toward the newspaper men and photographers. Everyone started speaking all at once.

'Please,' I managed to say to the woman who was hugging me and smiling at the photographers — the woman called

Diana Hamilton. 'I must find the police. I saw a girl being abducted.'

One would have thought I made a comment on the weather. Diana kept smiling. If she heard me she didn't show any evidence of it. She was too intent upon posing for the photographers and reporters swarming about us.

She forced me about to face another bank of flashing cameras and, turning me toward a distinguished-looking gentleman directly beside her, she said with a regal wave of her hand, 'Your stepfather, my dear.'

'Alice,' the man said, reaching his hand out to me. 'We're so happy you've come to stay with us.'

My mind was a complete blur. I didn't really see him or feel the touch of his hand. If she had said his name I wouldn't have heard it. People were smiling, talking, laughing. I was looking past all of them — or trying to. My frustration grew.

The conductor called, 'All aboard' and the train began to chug out of the station. Too much time had passed. The girl was gone by now. There would be no way of pursuing her or her captor at this point in time. It was too late. I found myself glowering at Diana Hamilton.

With a toss of her head she tucked my arm in hers and said, 'Come, my dear.' My stepfather took my other arm and between them they led me toward a line of automobiles parked outside a small, dilapidated waiting room. People were still scurrying around asking questions, taking pictures.

It confused me terribly, but Diana Hamilton was in her element, calm and aloof and very much in control of the situation. She answered the reporters slowly and clearly. She did not let the constant flashing of the bulbs disturb or distract her. She smiled. She hugged me from time to time as we walked along.

I said absolutely nothing. She chattered on but I heard not a word of it. Whatever questions were asked of me, Diana chose to answer on my behalf. How useless I felt.

When we reached the cars Diana nodded toward an older model Town Car. 'I do apologize, my dear. I'm afraid the chauffeur had a bit of trouble with the limousine at the last minute so we were obliged to take Leland's car. Alice and I will sit in the back, Leland.'

Leland got behind the wheel after Diana and I were seated in the back seat. Suddenly I remembered my baggage.

'My luggage,' I said as the crowd of faces peered into the car at us, still shouting questions, still taking flash pictures. Diana was pretending they weren't there, but her expression said otherwise.

'We'll send Martin for it later. It will be safe at the station. In a place like Gulf Point there is little fear it will be lost.'

Leland carefully backed the car out of the parking area and turned westward toward the Gulf. It was only after we were well away from the newspaper people that Diana allowed herself to relax. She fumbled in her purse for a cigarette, but she merely toyed with it without lighting it.

'Now, what is this you said about seeing a girl abducted?' Her voice was cold as ice. There was obvious disbelief in her tone.

'Yes, I saw it from the window of the train. The girl was racing across a field. A man in a chauffeur's uniform caught up to her and knocked her unconscious.'

'Perhaps you imagined it,' Diana said. 'The plane crash and all . . . '

'No, I saw it. I did not imagine it. I couldn't have imagined it.'

Leland glanced over his shoulder. 'The sun and shadows at this time of morning can be quite deceptive.'

'No. I saw it all quite clearly,' I insisted. I glanced at Diana and at once I understood.

She lived in a world of fantasy. She was used to imagining things and being surrounded by people with very active imaginations. For all I knew, Leland was part of that world too.

Diana gave a little laugh. 'Well, if you think it will make you feel better, we'll telephone the authorities when we reach home.'

'Do you honestly think that's necessary, my dear?' Leland asked.

'We must humor Alice,' she said in a condescending voice. 'I see no harm in Alice's reporting whatever it is she thinks she saw.'

Leland sighed and shrugged. 'I suppose not,' he agreed.

'You honestly feel that it is something you should report?' Diana asked me.

'Yes, I do,' I said firmly.

Of course I had to report it. I had to do something. I just couldn't witness the abduction of a poor unconscious girl and say nothing.

I bit down on my lower lip. Or perhaps it was nothing at all. Maybe the girl was merely some rich, precocious brat who was making a rebellious stand against her parents. It might well be very innocent.

The man had hit her, though. Regardless of how precocious the girl might be, I could see no earthly reason for a grown man knocking a defenseless child unconscious. Surely the man's employer didn't condone such treatment of his daughter — if he knew.

Diana sighed. She said no more; there was nothing to say. And we were both well aware of that fact. We may have been mother and daughter, but we were total strangers and lived in entirely different worlds.

She leaned into the far corner of the seat and threw back the veil of her hat. My quick glance turned into an open stare. She was old, much older than I had thought. The skin was loose and sagging. Her eyes were bright but the skin surrounding them was dark and wrinkled, although carefully camouflaged by eye make-up. The lines at the mouth were etched deep into the corners. The cheeks were shallow under the bright rouge. Her hat did a thorough job of hiding her hair, but I imagined that it was very evenly colored with that flat, solid look dyed hair takes on.

My surprise at seeing the real Diana Hamilton did not go unnoticed. She smiled a slow, careful smile and chuckled softly. There was something sad in her laugh. She tried to stare me down. I couldn't let her do that. I had to show her that I was as strong as she. I refused to let her intimidate me.

Finally she relented. She lifted the cigarette to her lips and brought the lighter to it, exhaling noisily. She leveled her eyes on me again. 'You didn't realize how old I am,' she said bluntly. 'I was thirty-three when you were born. I have more or less retired from public life. The camera can be both friend and enemy, both kind and malicious. In the past few years I came to realize how much it disliked me. I decided it was time for our relationship to come to an abrupt end. I am Mrs. Leland Braddock now. Diana Hamilton has ceased to exist. Unfortunately your untimely appearance forced Diana Hamilton back into the public's eyes for a brief time.' She waved her cigarette as though it were a magic wand. 'But that will change very soon.'

'I had no hand in what happened,' I said evenly. 'I was unconscious during those days they tried to find out who I was. I am just as displeased with this whole affair as you are. You needn't have sent for me, you know.'

'Of course I had to send for you. I had

no other alternative.' She stabbed out her cigarette.

Then suddenly her face went soft and her eyes turned more gentle. She reached out and patted my hand. 'But let us not quarrel, Alice. I realize none of this could have been avoided. It was time we met anyway. As it is, I've put off meeting you for too long a time.' She smiled and for a moment I thought the smile was genuine. 'I am really quite pleased that we can be together again.'

I almost believed her for a second.

I saw her eyes move to the back of her husband's head. Her expression suddenly changed again. 'Of course Falcon Island is an isolated spot. I'm afraid you will tire of it quickly and want to return home.'

I got the message clearly enough. 'I have no intentions of staying very long,' I said.

She nodded and said nothing.

Of course I'd known that I wasn't welcome at Falcon Island . . . wherever that was. I looked about at the landscape to see if I could get my bearings. I didn't want to talk any more. I hadn't really paid any attention to the scenery when we first started away from the train station at Gulf Point. We had since left that little town far behind us.

Now I looked around and reveled in the beauty of the place. Summer had just given spring an impatient nudge and everywhere I looked evidence of summer's reasons for that impatient nudge could be seen. I could almost feel the yellows and blues, the purples, the reds, the greens, the colors of summer. Already the days seemed brighter, hotter, although this was only the second day of the new season. The trees all looked so smooth and lush, so filled with shade and beauty, so young and alive. The land was flat and spacious and teeming with life and the vitality of nature.

Out of the corner of my eye I saw Diana studying my face. 'You know,' she said, 'you look very much like your father.'

How like her, I thought. My father used to tell me precisely the opposite. He said I was the spitting image of my mother. I used to compare myself to her magazine pictures. I could never convince myself, however, that I was or could ever be as beautiful as the famous Diana Hamilton, though there was definitely a resemblance. I had Diana's eyes, her delicate nose, the regal chin. I had very few of my father's features, except that I'd inherited his straight brown hair and his inquisitive nature.

Her gaze moved over me very slowly, very carefully. I could feel disdain radiating from her. She didn't like me any more than I cared for her. I could see both our reasons and understood them readily enough. To her, I represented proof of her maturity. To me, she represented a woman who had never wanted me. And she still did not want me. I could tell by the way she looked at me that she wanted me to go away and stay away.

There was something else, however: there was fear in her eyes. I couldn't imagine why she was afraid. There was something she was hiding and it was much more important than simply her true age. She lit another cigarette and exhaled the smoke in a heavy puff. 'You don't like me much, do you Alice?'

'Should I?' I asked, careful to keep my eyes focused on the scenery outside. I didn't want her to see the moisture that suddenly threatened to become tears.

I heard her sigh again. 'No, I guess not.'

We drove in silence. After a mile or two the trees that separated the road from the open fields fell back and the land opened up briefly, but no more than a mile later we were again engulfed in tall oaks and magnolias, red cypress and yellow pines, gums and hickories. Low tangles of Carolina yellow jasmine, Cherokee rose, and trumpet creepers made it difficult to see the ground itself.

'You've fully recovered from the plane crash, I presume,' Leland said over his shoulder.

'Yes, thank you, except, of course, for my leg. The doctor said the cast will have to stay on for quite a while.'

'I had a broken leg once, Leland,' Diana said, taking his attention immediately away from me. 'Did you know that?'

'No, dear, I didn't.'

'Yes. I broke it during the filming of that Bronte picture. Uhhh . . . you know . . . ' She snapped her fingers impatiently.

'*Wuthering Heights*,' Leland provided.

'Yes, that's the one. I fell from a rock.' Suddenly she laughed. 'It cost the studio a fortune. The way they carried on, one would have thought I broke the bone on purpose.' She turned suddenly to me. 'Did you enjoy me in *Wuthering Heights?*' she asked with her usual imperious smile.

Of course I'd seen the picture. Diana Hamilton had received an Academy Award for it. Yet, in spite of myself, I said, 'I don't recall seeing it.'

The look she gave me would easily have frozen water.

Again silence took over inside the car.

We passed through a patch of tropical forest. Cattleya orchids flourished everywhere, it seemed, their velvety vibrant petals drooping in sad dejection. Giant rafflesia measuring at least three feet across stretched out to catch whatever light they could in their massive circular raspberry-colored leaves. I saw marshmallow flowers with their rounded, pale pink petals and notch-edged leaves that came into sharp points. Magnolia and red-bud, and flame vines grew in tangles; lichens struggled to reach the sky. The whole place was exotic and yet frightening and oppressive.

As suddenly as the dark, dank forest had swallowed us up, it cast us out. The road widened, the bright sunlight poured down over us as Leland picked up speed. We were, I saw, on a coastline. Open water stretched out before us as far as the eye could see. Interrupting the expanse of water was a large island situated a mile or two from shore. The coastline itself was completely flat and bare, except for a low slung building hugging the water's edge.

Leland nodded out toward the sea. 'Falcon Island,' he said. 'It's been in my family for generations.'

'Whose house is that, on the shore there?'

'That?' He laughed. 'No one's house, that's a combination garage and boat house.'

I looked out over the water, in the direction he had indicated for Falcon

Island. I could see nothing but a blur in the distance. I saw no house, just the dark colors of trees and undergrowth. It looked most foreboding.

Leland slowed the car and headed toward the boat house. Its doors suddenly opened automatically. Just as we started into the garage I gasped. There, parked in the adjacent parking stall was an old-fashioned limousine — the type usually associated with stars of the silent screen. It was lavishly ornamented, shiny and polished and dripping with chrome plate.

I had seen it before. It was the car to which the brutish chauffeur had recently carried the unconscious girl.

2

'That car,' I gasped, staring at the antique limousine. 'That's the car the girl was carried off in.'

Diana fumbled with the veil on her hat. 'You're talking nonsense, Alice.'

'I'm not,' I said defiantly. 'I couldn't make a mistake about a car like that.'

I saw Diana and Leland exchange glances in the rear view mirror.

Diana turned on me. She looked angry. 'I don't know what you saw, or claimed to have seen, back in Gulf Point, but I can assure you, my dear, that the limousine has been here at the landing since yesterday afternoon. Martin has been working on the motor. The car isn't operable.' Her eyes glinted at me.

'But I know what I saw,' I insisted.

Leland was out of the car, holding open the back door for Diana and me. It was the same limousine; I was positive of it. I knew what I had seen and no one was going to convince me otherwise.

Diana was glaring at me. 'I do hope you are not insinuating that our chauffeur goes around spiriting away young, defenseless girls.'

'I know what I saw,' I said, but there wasn't as much defiance or conviction in my voice as I had wanted.

'Really, Alice, you're being impossible.' She got out of the car.

With the help of Leland and my crutch I climbed out after her and stood looking at the old limousine. I hadn't been mistaken. This was the very same car I saw back in the open field.

'This way, Alice,' Leland said softly, touching my elbow.

We rounded the garage and started toward a speedboat moored at the landing. 'If it will make you feel better, Alice,' Leland said as we straggled along behind the imperious Diana Hamilton, 'we'll speak to Martin when we get to the house. Perhaps he allowed a friend to borrow the car.'

'Thank you,' I said, smiling at him. I

felt he was on my side, or at least trying to be.

Diana clambered into the boat without assistance. Diana Hamilton, I felt, never needed assistance from anyone. She had made her own way all of her life and the mere idea of her getting old didn't break that habit. Changing her name to Braddock had obviously not affected her; she was and would always be Diana Hamilton, no matter how many husbands she'd had. And she'd had a few, I thought, remembering the gossip columns and fan magazine articles I'd read. Five — and Leland Braddock made six.

She didn't rise to help me when I dropped my crutch and almost tripped into the speedboat. Leland grabbed me before I had a chance to fall. Diana merely looked annoyed. She was not the type woman who tolerated weakness of any kind. She kept her head averted until I'd seated myself beside her.

Leland took the controls, Diana and I behind him on the double seat. He backed the speedboat away from the landing and turned it toward the open water.

No one spoke on the trip across; the roar of the motor made conversation difficult. For this I was glad. It gave me the chance I needed to gather my wits about me and instill resolve back into my mind.

Falcon Island loomed on the horizon ahead of us like a beckoning specter. It looked dark and misty from this distance and I saw no signs of a house anywhere, just a line of trees that butted the sea. Overhead the sky was clear and blue with puffy white clouds scattered here and there. Under other circumstances I would have leaned back and reveled in the beauty of my surroundings, but I couldn't relax and enjoy myself. I wanted to be back in Hillsborough where I belonged. I wanted to stand in front of my schoolchildren and tell them about King Arthur, The Prince and the Pauper, The Little Match Girl. I wanted my simple unencumbered life back again. I didn't want the clutter of a famous mother, a stepfather I'd never seen or heard of, an island that was completely isolated from the entire world.

I was a victim of a happening. A plane crash. Five horrifying minutes of a plane-load of passengers plunging down, down, down and then nothing, blackness, utter and complete silence . . . only to awake to find myself in another existence.

I threw back my head and let the fresh sea air cleanse my thoughts. I pinched shut my eyes. I wouldn't think of the screams, the panic, the sounds of violent death. I wouldn't, I couldn't think of any of it.

Leland made a wide sweep to the left. I saw the trees fall back; we were approaching the island from a side that faced out toward the open sea. A sandy beach ran along this side of the island, looking smooth and warm and very inviting from this distance.

Now I could see Falcon House. It sat on a slight hill overlooking the trees, the beach, the sea itself. It was a rambling affair of many turrets, towers, cupolas, all painted a dismal gray, with trim of a still darker shade of gray, almost black.

Even at a distance, I could see it needed repairs — major repairs. The shutters on several windows drooped from their hinges, boards covered other windows and doorways, and here and there a roof that sagged. One cupola had even toppled over.

Why did Diana Hamilton insist upon living in a crumbling house? Surely money was no object. Leland Braddock was not young; he had to have money in order to attract the attention of such a celebrity as Diana Hamilton.

'It must have been lovely in its day,' I said, testing their reactions.

Leland had cut the motor and jumped out to tie up the boat. 'Yes, it was quite a show place at one time. Unfortunately it was never a good show place. Falcon House, like my lovely wife,' he said, smiling at Diana, 'dislikes publicity intensely. They've both had more than their share and are now content just to live out their lives in anonymity.'

Diana gave us both a frosty look. 'Unfortunately we cannot always do what we choose,' she said.

'Never mind, darling,' he said pleasantly, putting out his hand to help me from the boat.

Again Diana got out without assistance. Once on the jetty Leland put his arm around her waist. I saw her stiffen briefly before she relaxed against him.

He patted her tenderly. 'This thing will all blow over in a couple of days,' he said.

'I hope so,' she answered, almost to herself.

Leland turned to me and saw me struggling with my crutch. 'Here, let me help. That thing must be most difficult to manipulate.'

'I'm getting rather used to it, really,' I said, hobbling along beside them.

A man in a chauffeur's uniform hurried toward the landing to meet us. He was bareheaded, with silver-blond tussled hair; his face was square, Germanic, and his features looked as though they'd been chiseled out of stone.

'Oh, Martin,' Diana said. 'My — Miss Whelan's bags are at the station at Gulf Point. Is the limousine repaired? Can you go and fetch them?'

I thought I saw the slightest glimmer of a question pass across the chauffeur's face. 'Yes, ma'am,' he answered. He turned and looked at me. 'May I help, Miss?' he asked.

I backed away, staring up at him. The build, the features, the look of him — he had been wearing a cap when I first saw him, but there was no mistaking it, this was the same man who dashed after the young girl. This was the man I saw knock that girl unconscious.

Leland noticed my staring at him.

'Martin?' he said. 'Miss Whelan believes she saw the limousine near Gulf Point a while ago. Had you taken the car out to test it, or did you perhaps lend it to someone?'

Martin gave him a look that said absolutely nothing. 'No, sir,' he answered. 'The car has been at the boathouse since yesterday. No one borrowed it, Mr. Braddock.' He searched in the pocket of his jacket. 'I have the keys,' he added, producing the ignition key and holding it up for all of us to see.

'Yes, yes,' Leland said, clearing his

throat. 'Miss Whelan must have been mistaken,' he added with an uncomfortable shrug of his shoulders.

'I was not mistaken,' I said with determination. 'I saw what I saw. That limousine was used to spirit away a young girl.'

Martin turned his icy eyes on me. 'I'm afraid you must be mistaken, Miss. The car hasn't been away from the landing.'

'And I am also certain I saw you with that young girl,' I accused.

'Alice, really,' Diana exploded. 'I must insist that you put a stop to this ridiculous nonsense. I remind you that you are a guest in this house and I will not have you making such insane accusations of our servants.'

I couldn't be certain, but I thought I saw Martin flinch at the word 'servants.'

Diana turned to the chauffeur. 'My daughter has been in a horrible airplane crash,' she explained. 'She isn't quite herself as yet.'

I opened my mouth to defend myself but Diana narrowed her eyes. She warned me with one simple word. 'Alice!'

There was something very wrong in this place, I told myself. I watched Martin turn and go toward a second power boat that was docked at the jetty. He glanced back over his shoulder at me, but other than that gave no outward sign of feeling disturbed by my accusation.

I was angry, more at myself than anyone else. I should not have been so bold as to come right out and display my suspicions about Martin and the car. I would have been cleverer if I were Diana Hamilton. She wouldn't have voiced her thoughts. She would have investigated in private until she was sure of everything and then pointed an accusing finger.

Well, if I had to play that game I would. I knew I'd seen Martin hit a young girl and carry her away in the limousine. To where? I didn't know, but that girl might well be here in this house, on this island. I knew now that I'd get no assistance from Diana or Leland. Despite all their efforts of making me believe I imagined the whole affair, I felt intent upon proving them wrong.

As I stood there beside her I felt I had

to show my mother that I was as strong and as determined as she. I was positive I was right. They were hiding something. But if that were so, why did they bring me here?

Or had they no other choice? It was obvious that Diana didn't want me and possibly it wasn't for the reasons I'd originally thought. Perhaps Diana Hamilton had something hidden in her life that might be exposed by my presence. But what?

The young girl I'd seen racing across the field? Who was she? Where did she fit into this puzzle?

I shook my head. Or was I being overly dramatic. It was possible the girl was just a romantic entanglement of Martin's. She could well have been older than she looked to me. I'd been a distance away when I saw him hit her. Still, he had hit her. He'd knocked her unconscious. Even if she were a girl friend of Martin's, he had no right to abuse her in that manner.

Martin had lied. I could tell by his eyes that he lied when he said the car was at the landing since yesterday.

And he knew I knew he was lying.

3

My thoughts were so taken up with Martin and the limousine that I almost didn't notice the surroundings through which we were walking. Like the house, the grounds were in a terrible state of neglect. The grass was uncut, the hedges untended. A thick forest of trees and brush bordered the house like a horse-shoe, the open space being occupied by the sandy beach which, now that I saw it up close, was littered with driftwood and gnat-attracting clumps of slick kelp.

We went up a brick stairway that needed fixing. Weeds had pushed up between the cracks to catch the sun. We skirted a huge swimming pool that had obviously gone unused for many years. It was drained of water, its tiles were cracked and crumbling, dirt and leaves covered its bottom.

Another brick walk in the same state of disrepair took us up onto a wide terrace that ran across the full front of the house. This, at least, looked as if it were used from time to time. Bright multi-striped umbrellas shaded metal tables and chairs. The marble flooring was swept clean — but not scrubbed. The sun chaises were new looking. I wondered briefly if they'd been recently purchased for my benefit. No, I decided, glancing at my famous mother; she wasn't the type of woman who did anything to impress another woman, not even her own daughter.

The mansion towered over us, larger than I had at first thought. Jasmine and purple bougainvillea hung from the tiled roof, and every cornice was unattractively splattered with birds' droppings. The riotous natural growth that seemed to invade every part of the exterior made it evident that nature was merely waiting to claim its rightful heritage.

I paused on the terrace, looking about, pretending to catch my breath. I thought I saw movement at one of the upstairs windows, and glanced up. A shadow passed across the curved window of the tower at the south corner. The second floor section of the south tower had no outside wall; one massive window ran completely around the outer curve of the tower. It surprised me somewhat to see so massive a window in such perfect state of repair. Even the tower itself seemed to be better maintained than the whole rest of the house.

'What's that?' I asked Leland, pointing up to the glass-fronted tower.

Again Leland and Diana exchanged a strange fleeting glance.

'Just an old solarium,' Leland told me. 'My grandmother was quite a plant nut, like me.' He chuckled but it was a mirthless chuckle.

'You?'

'Yes, plants are a hobby of mine,' he said. He looked up at the glass front. 'The solarium is never used any more. I'm afraid I'm letting the place go to pot.'

I was going to comment on the good condition of the south tower, but instead I said, 'Why? It's such a beautiful place . . . or at least it could be.'

'The house is too old. It isn't worth

fixing. The repairs would cost more than the property is worth.' He sighed, looking wistful. 'Someday the whole place will fall down around our heads and Diana and I will be forced to find a new home, but until that time we like to think of this as home. We like it here, believe it or not.'

Diana turned and went inside. Leland motioned toward the front door. 'I believe you'll find the interior a little less depressing,' he said.

Leland was wrong. The interior was just as depressing as the outside, although I had to admit that it looked better cared for. The main hall was paneled in dark, dull wood. The staircase that led to the upper floors was a strange, square affair, going off at all sorts of crazy angles, like a patchwork quilt.

We were in the center of the house, I thought. I looked around and saw doorways — all in dark oak panels and all closed — that went off into rooms on both sides. The entrance hall was completely empty except for a marble topped console table that supported a huge burst of pampas grass, dry and dead looking.

'Have you had breakfast, my dear?' Diana asked as she slipped off her hat and gloves and tossed them on the console next to her handbag.

'Yes, on the train,' I told her.

'Then perhaps you'd like to go directly to your room and rest for a while? We'll have lunch on the terrace in about an hour or so.'

I noticed she did not offer to sit and chat. We hadn't seen each other in over twenty years and she was treating me like someone she saw every day. Casual little comments, admonitions, small talk. There was no attempt at friendliness, no display of affection, or pleasure at seeing me.

To be truthful, I was rather glad. I knew her attempts would only be artificial and I would not have welcomed any such shows of emotion.

'I am a little tired,' I told her.

'Then come along,' Diana answered, squaring her shoulders and walking toward a small door tucked away under the stairs. She pressed a button and the door slid open to reveal a private elevator. I breathed an inward sigh of relief, knowing I wouldn't have to tackle that crazy staircase.

When the door to the small lift closed and I found myself alone for the first time with my mother, I felt a tinge of uneasiness. She was looking at me, eyeing me from head to foot.

'We will try to make you comfortable while you are here,' she said.

'Thank you,' I answered, hoping I sounded as aloof as she. 'I can't stay very long, you know, I have my job to think about.'

'Oh, yes. They tell me you teach school, or some such thing.'

Her snobbishness was irritating. 'Some such thing,' I answered as sarcastically as I could.

Diana jabbed a button. The elevator gave a little jolt and we started upward. 'I rather hoped that we could be friends,' she said after a while.

I merely looked at her.

'It has all been very difficult for me,' she went on. 'You have no idea how dearly I've wanted to have you with me. Of course, you know my career would never permit that.'

'Oh, Mother, please, since when does one's career take precedence over one's own flesh and blood?' I could feel the stinging behind my eyes, but I refused to let the tears come. I wouldn't show her how much I'd missed her during all those long, lonely years. I wouldn't show her that she'd hurt me terribly — could still hurt me if she chose to.

The elevator thumped to a halt on the second level. The door swooshed open. Diana swept out of the lift, leaving me to manage on my own.

'You can't possibly understand my position, can you, Alice?' she asked over her shoulder as we walked slowly down the wide hallway. Like the entrance hall, the corridor was paneled in dark, dull wood and was as depressing as what I'd seen of the house so far.

'No, I can't.'

'It is a great responsibility, being famous. One can't think of oneself, or do what one most pleases. I lived for those faces out there in the dark — hundreds and hundreds of faces who came to me in order to try and forget their drab, dreary existences. I was only a child when I started in movies during the depression years, and during those dark times I came to realize just how much my face, my pictures meant to millions of starving people.'

She stood before a door — presumably the door to the room assigned to me, but she made no move to open it. She turned and faced me. 'I never forgot the letters I received during those years, letters in which untold millions poured out their hearts to me, told me how important I was to them, how much they needed me in order to forget about their bleak reality, if only for a short time. Yes,' she said, nodding her head gravely. 'I have always been known as a hard, ruthless woman, but I have had to be hard and ruthless because I had to exist. Not for myself, but for them, my public.'

I stood there staring at her. For a moment I thought she was merely play-acting, but when I looked closely into her face I saw something that told me otherwise. Dedication was written all over her. Her eyes gleamed and sparkled when she said, ' . . . for them, my public.'

She made a humble little gesture with her hands, and pushing open the door to my room, stood back and let me enter before her.

I crossed the room without seeing it and went directly to the windows and looked out over the sea beyond the forest. I could feel her presence at my back. I knew without turning that she was standing in the open doorway, one hand holding on to the knob.

'Alice,' she said softly. 'Please try not to hate me too much. I only did what I thought was best for you.'

I whirled around. 'Best for me,' I said sharply, feeling the tears begin to form at my lids. 'How could you possibly know what was good for me? You don't know me at all. You never tried to know me. You could have sent for me after Daddy died, but no, you chose to keep me hidden away in private schools.'

She didn't flinch. 'And what kind of a

life would you have had if I had sent for you? Your schooling would have been seriously neglected, your life would have been one of constant moving about, losing friends, change, change, change. How would a little girl of six cope with a life like that?' Her voice wasn't raised, it was calm and well under control. 'I know only too well how that type life can harm a little girl. No, Alice. I believe I did the right thing. You may not agree with that, but my conscience is clear. I *know* I did the right thing.'

'The right thing for you perhaps,' I said in a choked voice. I turned back to the windows so that she wouldn't see the tears.

She said nothing for a while. I thought she was going to close the door and leave the discussion right there. She didn't. 'I admit that your life wasn't all it should have been, but I am convinced that I did what was best for both of us.'

I put my head down and tried to keep my shoulders still.

'Get some rest, Alice. I'm afraid this conversation is only upsetting us both. I shouldn't have started it, but it was inevitable. It's best that we both know where we stand.'

I heard the door click shut and the silence of the room overpowered me. The emptiness that engulfed me was awesome. I spun away from the windows and threw myself across the bed. Whether or not Diana heard me crying I didn't know, and I didn't care.

How could she expect me to believe her? I asked myself, pounding my fists into the coverlet. Even after our long, unnecessary separation, she still didn't want me. She still made it clear that I was not welcome to stay on in this house with her. She didn't want me as a child and she didn't want me as a woman. She could make all the pretty little speeches she wanted to, but the fact remained that I was not welcome here. She'd send me away, just as she'd sent me away years and years ago.

I wouldn't think kindly toward her — I wouldn't, I kept telling myself. Yet there was an ache deep inside me which I couldn't ignore. Despite all the hurt, all the disappointments I'd suffered at her hands, I still looked upon her as my mother. I still considered myself her daughter and I wanted her to love me as much as I wanted to love her.

What will crying accomplish? I asked myself, purposely brushing away the tears and sitting up on the bed. I'd cried enough.

'At least I'll have privacy here,' I said as I looked around.

I got up and went back to the windows. I sighed. Outside the sun shimmered on the distant water. I tried not to look down at the thick tangle of woods that was immediately beneath my window. They had put me in the north wing of the house, I noticed, glancing up at the direction of the sun.

I pushed open the window and let the cool sea breezes dry the tears on my cheeks. I heard what I thought was a motorboat and glanced back toward the sea. I was right. A small power launch skimmed across the waters, headed toward Falcon Island. It didn't look like the same boat Martin had taken. Bright yellow, it looked like a sunbeam dancing over the waves. I saw it swerve and turn inward toward the beach. It disappeared but I could hear its motor continue to purr in the distance. Then the motor stopped.

The thought of a speedboat — of Martin — brought back my determination to get to the root of my mystery. I pushed Diana out of my head and glanced around the room. A telephone sat on the nightstand next to the bed. I went to it and picked up the receiver.

'May I help you?' an operator asked after I dialed.

'Would you connect me with the Police Department in Gulf Point, please?'

'There is no Police Department there, Miss. Will the Sheriff's Office do?'

'Yes, thank you.'

My hand felt clammy as I clutched the receiver tight to my ear. I wondered if anyone could possibly know I was using the telephone. I felt guilty about not having asked permission, and yet I didn't care.

'Sheriff's Office.'

'Yes. My name is Alice Whelan, I'm Diana Hamilton's daughter.'

The man on the other end must have smiled. He sounded pleased. 'Oh, yes, Miss Whelan. Some of my men were down at the station when you arrived this morning. How's your mother?'

I scowled. Always the same question. Never once did anyone ask about me. After all, I was the one who was almost killed in that plane crash.

'She's fine, thank you,' I said, trying hard to keep my voice controlled. 'What I'm calling about is something I saw in Gulf Point this morning. It's been bothering me terribly.'

'And what might that be?' he asked with a chuckle. 'Did the local reporters give you a bad time?'

'No, nothing like that.' I screwed up my courage. 'I saw a girl knocked unconscious and carried away.'

There was a dead silence on the other end of the line. I just heard him breathing. Then he said, 'And just where did you see this happen, Miss Whelan?'

'Just as the train was pulling into the

station. I saw it out of my compartment window.'

'I see.' He sounded as though he were making notes, but then he put his hand partially over the mouthpiece and started to talk to someone in the background. 'It's that Whelan girl,' I heard him say. 'The one who was in the plane crash.'

I heard someone mutter an answer.

The hand slipped a little from the mouthpiece. 'She claims she saw a girl abducted at Gulf Point station.'

Laughter. 'Her stepfather was right then,' I heard the voice in the background say, most clearly. 'He called and said we might be hearing from her with some cock-and-bull story. Shock from the accident, he said.'

The man came back on the line. 'This morning, you say?'

'Please,' I said, losing my control. 'I am not imagining it. I saw a chauffeur hit a girl and knock her unconscious. Then he threw her into a limousine and sped away.'

'Yes, I see.'

But I could tell he didn't see. He was humoring me.

'Well, we'll look into it, Miss Whelan. Now you just calm yourself and get a lot of rest, you hear?'

My frustration was beginning to grow.

'And tell your mother that Sheriff Anderson conveys his regards.'

He hung up and left me standing there listening to a dead line.

I wanted to scream.

4

I was glad it was Leland who came to summon me to lunch. How dare he hint to the authorities that I was suffering from shock and having hallucinations? The moment I opened my bedroom door and saw him standing there, I lost my temper. The smile he wore faded when he noticed my look of anger.

'Alice. What's the matter?'

'How dare you insinuate to the sheriff that I'm mentally disturbed?' I fumed.

His mouth fell open. 'What?'

'I telephoned the sheriff's office to report seeing that girl abducted. You'd already called and warned them that I might do something like that — that I'm suffering from shock and I am imagining things.'

'Alice, dear. Calm yourself. I don't know what you're talking about.'

'Oh, don't you? I heard them say you called about me.'

He looked truly surprised. 'The sheriff told you I called him?'

'No, not the sheriff; someone in the background. The sheriff had his hand over the mouthpiece, but I could hear. A man said you called and warned them that I was suffering from shock, that my mind wasn't quite right.'

'There, there, my dear. You must have misunderstood. Why would I call the sheriff and say such a thing?'

He looked so innocent, so sincere that for a brief moment I found myself doubting my own ears. I shook my head violently. 'No, I heard them. They were laughing at me.' All of a sudden, without any warning at all, I burst into tears. I sank into a chair, burying my face in my hands and gave myself up to my frustration.

He patted my shoulder. 'Alice, you must calm yourself. We all know what a terrible ordeal you've been through. I didn't call anyone. I haven't used the telephone since we returned from Gulf Point. I'm telling you the truth, my dear. Try and believe me.'

'Then who?' I sobbed. 'Who would do such a cruel thing?'

'I don't think anyone did. I'm not saying you imagined hearing what you thought you heard, I'm only saying that perhaps you misunderstood the words. Surely the conversation was muffled . . . you just didn't hear distinctly, that's all.' He paused, then asked, 'What did the sheriff say when you told him about what you'd seen?'

I tried to get myself back into control. Was Leland right? Had I misunderstood? I tried to bring back the conversation, tried to remember the exact words, but it was all a blur now.

Finally I straightened my back. No, I wasn't imagining things. I wasn't suffering from shock. I had to control myself. After a moment I wiped away my tears with the back of my hand. Leland fumbled for a handkerchief and handed it to me.

I lowered my head and said meekly, 'The sheriff said they'd check into it.'

'There. See. Now what more can you ask for? You told him what you saw and he said they'd check it out. And I'm sure they will.' He tried to help me from the chair. 'Come along, child. Let's have a nice lunch. We'll eat out on the terrace. The sun is bright and warm and it's a glorious day. And there is someone here who's anxious to meet you.'

I suddenly remembered the speedboat I'd heard approaching the island. Who was it? I wasn't in any mood to meet anyone new. I was so tired of people, people, people. The last several weeks had been littered with new faces, all asking the same questions and talking about the same things — things I dearly wanted to forget.

'I don't feel up to meeting anyone,' I said.

'Of course you do. You'll enjoy Justin. He's bright and gay and charming. Come along. Fix yourself up. He'll help take your mind off things, and I made him promise he's not to mention the accident. Come along, child. Justin's one of the family. He's my younger brother and a very nice, ordinary guy.'

'Well, let me repair my face, Leland.

You go ahead. I'll find my own way down in a bit.'

'Now promise you won't disappoint us? And don't be too long. Diana doesn't like being kept waiting.'

I hobbled into the bathroom and put cold water on my face. I refused to let myself be hurried, regardless of whether my mother had to wait or not. I felt rebellion welling up inside me.

And I didn't believe Leland either. I had heard the sheriff and his deputy laughing. I'd heard what the other man said, too. Leland had lied.

Why? Why were they making such an issue out of this whole affair? The girl must be known to them. There was no doubt in my mind that the chauffeur I'd seen in Gulf Point had been Martin, their chauffeur. But who was the girl?

I admonished myself for having railed at Leland. Naturally he'd deny calling the sheriff; I should have known that. I remembered my promise to myself to investigate in secret; unfortunately I'd broken that promise already. I'd told Leland in so many words that I was still

55

intent upon finding out what happened to that girl.

That was a mistake. I had to pretend loss of interest in the matter. I knew now that if I ever intended getting to the bottom of this whole mess I'd have to do it on my own. Neither Leland nor my mother was going to be of any help; on the contrary, they'd be a hindrance.

I applied some lipstick, pinched color back into my cheeks and frowned at the puffiness under my eyes. I shrugged. I didn't care how I looked, really.

I heard voices when I got out of the lift. Diana was laughing. I'd heard her stage laugh at Gulf Point when she spoke to the reporters and photographers, but I'd never heard this laugh. It was real. She sounded genuinely happy.

Double doors which had been closed when we first arrived were now standing open. I went toward them and stood at the threshold of a bright, comfortable drawing room. Unlike the rest of the house, this room was delightful. Tall French windows opened onto the terrace. The room was done in vivid, happy colors

— yellows and oranges, greens and whites, the furniture French and expensive. Thick cream-colored carpeting ran from wall to wall and the walls themselves were covered in pale yellow silk. Unlike the rest of Falcon House, this room was alive.

Diana and Leland were seated side by side on one of the divans that flanked the fireplace. A man, his back to me, sat on the other divan.

'Ah, here she is now,' Diana said, smiling brightly as she got up and came toward me. She tucked my arm in hers and led me into the room.

'My daughter,' she announced — and I thought for a moment she said it with an element of pride.

Leland and the other man were on their feet.

'Feeling better?' Leland asked. For some reason the question irritated me. Was he trying to hint to this stranger that I was not well? I ignored his question.

'Alice, may I present Leland's brother, Justin. Justin Braddock, my daughter, Alice.'

I was accustomed to the handsome young men who came to Southern California to find their fortune in motion pictures — those sun gods with their bronzed bodies and trim, perfect physiques — I found beauty among the young somewhat commonplace.

Justin Braddock was far from commonplace. He was strikingly good looking. His mouth was full, but not overly so. His chin was square and closely shaven. He wore his dark hair a little on the shaggy side, which added to his masculinity.

His beautiful green eyes were taking me in with frank appraisal. The whole room seemed even brighter than before when he smiled at me. 'Alice,' he said, putting out his hand. 'I'm honored.'

Our gaze held. I saw nothing at all of Diana or Leland or the lovely drawing room. I could only see Justin Braddock.

'Mr. Braddock,' I managed to stammer.

'Here, let me help you,' he said, taking me from Diana and seating me alongside him on the divan. As his hand gripped my arm, electricity coursed through me. I felt my whole body begin to tremble slightly.

'We have something in common,' he said as we grouped ourselves around the fireplace.

I widened my smile and silently cursed the cast on my leg. It never looked more unsightly. 'Oh? And what might that be?' I asked.

'We both teach,' he said. 'Your mother tells me you teach school in California. So do I — but I mean here, of course.'

Diana got to her feet. 'We can talk about that another time,' she said, once again making herself the center of attention. But Justin Braddock's eyes never left mine. 'Come, Justin,' Diana said. 'You can take me into lunch.' She held out her hand to him.

Justin hesitated. 'But perhaps Alice would care for a noonday cocktail before lunch. I know I would,' he said. He glanced down at me and smiled again.

'Yes, that would be nice,' I said.

'Nonsense. You know I don't approve of alcoholic beverages until after six,' Diana said haughtily. 'It's bad for the heart. Anyway, I'm simply famished.

Leland, tell Hattie we're ready to sit down.'

I started to struggle to my feet. The cast had never felt more clumsy.

'Here, let me help you,' Justin said. 'That thing must weigh a ton.'

Diana stood there watching us. 'I can say from experience that they do,' she said before I had a chance to answer him. 'Alice truly amazes me with how well she can manage on her own.'

'I'm very accustomed to it,' I said. Would our battle never end?

'What do you teach?' I asked Justin as we straggled out onto the terrace.

'Botany. I'm at Carson College. It's only a stone's throw from here. I'm a regular freeloader at Falcon House.'

I liked Justin Braddock. He stated his mind. 'Carson College? I've never heard of it.'

'It's just a hole in the wall, but I like it.'

Diana seated herself. 'You are capable of so much more, Justin,' she said. 'Why you waste your time at Carson I'll never know.'

Justin merely shrugged. 'As I said, I like

it. I'm not out looking for any big success in life. I like what I do and I make a comfortable living. What else is there?'

'Family, children,' I tested.

'Oh, I intend to get around to all that stuff eventually.'

Diana unfolded a napkin on her lap. 'You mustn't wait much longer, Justin. You are already getting rather set in your ways, I've noticed.'

Again Justin merely shrugged as he helped me into a chair and seated himself beside me. 'I'm in no hurry. The right girl just hasn't come along so far.'

I thought I felt his eyes on me. I didn't dare look up to see whether or not I was right.

'I just don't have Leland's luck,' he said to Diana.

I saw her smile widen. That remark unruffled her feathers. Justin was smooth. I'd have to watch out for that polish of his.

'I'll take that as a compliment,' Diana said, preening.

'It was meant as one.'

I shifted uncomfortably in my chair.

Leland joined us, followed by a short, squat little woman with pure white hair and a scowl on her face. She wheeled a serving cart.

'Martin hasn't come back yet,' she said, complaining to Diana.

'You can manage, Hattie,' Diana answered with an impatient wave of her hand. 'You don't have all that much to do around here.'

'But Martin usually takes care of . . . '

'Hattie!' Leland barked.

They exchanged long, veiled looks. Hattie bent to the task of serving lunch and no one spoke for several minutes.

'Justin,' Diana said, her voice again light and rippling. 'You must take Alice boating one of these afternoons.' She turned her head to me. 'Would you like that, Alice?'

'Yes, very much,' I told her.

'Good. Perhaps we should all go. We could make a sort of picnic of it.'

Leland grunted. 'You verge on seasickness merely taking the trip from the mainland,' he told his wife.

The sound of a speedboat suddenly

broke into the conversation. We all turned and looked down toward the beach.

'There's Martin now,' Leland said as he tasted the crisp crab salad. 'It took him long enough, I must say.'

Diana ignored the comment and began telling Justin about the commotion everyone made when she went to meet my train this morning. I noticed she made no mention whatsoever of my having seen a girl abducted. I reminded myself of the promise I'd made my mirror. I said nothing.

Martin came toward us toting my luggage. As he came up onto the terrace, Hattie turned on him. 'It's high time,' she scolded.

He merely grunted and went on by.

'You know where they go,' Diana called after him.

'Yes, ma'am,' he said over his shoulder.

I waited until Hattie had finished serving and was gone from the terrace before I asked, 'Has Martin been with you long, Leland?'

'Quite a while. About fifteen years, I guess.'

'He hardly looks old enough,' I commented.

'He's a lot older than he looks,' Diana put in. 'He was with Leland before we married.'

'Long before,' Leland added.

'He's quite a guy,' Justin said. 'He must be close to forty-five, but he looks younger than me.'

'And how old are you?' I asked with a sly little grin.

'Old enough,' Justin answered with a laugh. Then he added, 'Thirty-six. How about you?'

'Twenty-four.'

'You don't look it,' we both said to each other in unison. We started to laugh.

Leland laughed with us. Diana did not.

'Ah, youth,' Leland said with a sigh. 'Remember, darling?'

'Really, Leland,' Diana said, 'You make us sound like antiques.'

I saw Justin give me a sly little look. I smiled back at him. I don't know whether Diana saw our exchange of glances, but she looked very put out.

'You know,' Justin said, turning toward

me. 'I had every intention of meeting your train myself this morning, but I got there too late. You were driving away in Leland's car just as I got to the station.' He paused and turned to Leland. 'Just out of curiosity, why didn't you let Martin drive you, Lee? I know how you hate to get behind the wheel of a car.'

'Martin was repairing the limousine,' Diana explained. 'There was something wrong with the motor.'

'How could that be?' Justin said. 'He left the station a little ahead of you all. I saw him.'

Diana dropped her fork.

'Impossible,' Leland said a little too loudly.

Justin made a nervous little noise down in his throat. 'Perhaps I was mistaken,' he said shamefacedly.

'You were,' Leland said firmly.

5

Justin looked annoyed with himself.

So Martin and the limousine were in Gulf Point this morning. I kept my eyes and my expression veiled and pretended to concentrate on my lunch. The quiet was almost unbearable as the four of us sat there, each consumed by his own thoughts.

And what had the old housekeeper intended saying before Leland cut her off? Who does Martin usually take care of?

There was someone else in this house. And I had a fairly good notion just who that someone else was. But why was the girl kept hidden away? What was everyone trying to conceal? My concern for the girl I'd seen at Gulf Point now turned into a downright obsession. Martin had spirited the young thing away — he had spirited her away to Falcon Island, to Falcon House. I was sure of it now. I'd have to watch for an opportunity to explore.

Justin made his excuses immediately after lunch and took his motorboat back across the gulf. He said he had some lab work to finish up, and since he had no classes tomorrow — Friday — he'd be back in the morning to spend a long weekend.

I spent the afternoon unpacking and making myself comfortable in my lonely little room. As I worked I tried to ignore the questions that plagued me. I had to bide my time. Eventually everything would become clear and all the pieces of the puzzle would fall into place.

As a pleasant diversion, I thought about Justin Braddock. He was nice — awfully nice — and I found myself wanting tomorrow to come quickly so that I could see him again.

Someone tapped loudly on my door and sent thoughts of Justin flying out the window.

'I'm Hattie,' the housekeeper announced in a booming voice when I opened the door. 'I'm supposed to see if you need any help.'

I found myself smiling at her dour expression. 'I'm Alice,' I said. 'Thank you, Hattie, but I know how busy you must be. I think I can manage.'

Her expression grew less hostile. She shifted her weight. 'I don't mind, Miss Alice. I have a couple of minutes I can spare.'

She went over, to one of my empty suitcases. 'I'll just put this in the box room,' she said. 'You want these pressed out?' She scooped up two or three dresses I'd flung over the end of the bed.

'Yes, but I can do that if you'll bring me an iron.'

'Nonsense. It's not that much trouble.' She stood there with the dresses hanging over one arm. 'Is the room okay? I did as best I could getting it ready.'

'It's fine, Hattie. Just fine. I know I'll be comfortable.' I hesitated, and said, idly, 'This is a terribly large house. Do you take care of it all alone?'

'Martin helps,' she said, 'but not much.'

'Is there only my mother and Mr. Leland living here?'

I saw her brows knit together. She was eyeing me suspiciously. 'Sure,' she said, keeping her eyes narrowed at me. 'Who else should there be?'

I gave an uncomfortable shrug of my shoulders. 'It's just that it seems so large just for two people.'

'Most of it's boarded up, except for this wing and . . . ' She didn't finish her sentence. She looked as though she was biting down on her tongue. She fumbled with the dresses. 'Well, I'll get these pressed up for you. I'll have them back in no time.'

'There isn't any hurry, Hattie. And please don't let me be a bother.'

She made a little grunting sound and started to leave. At the doorway she hesitated again and turned back. She stood there looking at me for a minute then said, 'I wouldn't go wandering about in this old place. It isn't too safe.' She turned abruptly and left me standing there looking after her.

I found myself frowning. Why had she said that? Why had she warned me about roaming around? Perhaps it was only because the house was in such a terrible state of disrepair. Nevertheless, I was more than ever convinced there was someone else in this house and I was also pretty sure I knew who that someone was.

★ ★ ★

Dinner that evening was a simple affair, held in a large, drafty dining room off the main entrance hall. We had cocktails first in a tiny, drab little sitting room next to the dining hall. As usual, Diana held the reins of conversation in her capable hands; Leland was unusually quiet. He said hardly a word all during the cocktails and dinner. Diana, on the other hand, rambled on about everything and nothing, but I could easily see that her mind wasn't on anything she said. She gave Leland nervous little glances from time to time.

'I know I'm being a terrible host,' Leland said as we lingered over coffee, 'but I'm afraid you'll have to excuse me. I'm feeling unusually tired this evening.'

'You go along, Leland,' Diana said. 'I'll

be up directly. I'm sure Alice herself could do with a good night's sleep. We've all had a difficult day.' She got to her feet. It was obvious that dinner was over and I was being sent to my room.

The three of us went up in the little elevator together. Diana walked me to the door of my room. 'Good night, Alice dear,' she said kissing my cheek. 'Now get yourself straight into bed. Is there anything I can do for you?'

'No, I'm fine, thank you,' I said. 'I may read for a while.'

'You shouldn't, Alice. You're looking most tired. I'd feel it a personal favor if you'd get a really good night's sleep. Promise?' she said, giving me a pleading look. She was being overly charming. I didn't really mind; I rather liked it in fact.

I nodded. 'All right. I'll see you in the morning.'

'Leland and I usually sleep quite late. If you're up before us just ring for Hattie. She'll fix you some breakfast. And Justin should be here about eleven. You'll entertain him for us if we're still in bed, won't you?'

'Of course,' I said, and found myself smiling.

We bade each other good night. There was no embracing.

I sat in the window seat gazing out over the tops of the trees. The sea shimmered and glistened under the light of the moon and the air seemed to hang heavy and still over the island, as though a storm might be brewing. The hour was early and I was far from tired, although I knew I should be. Someone tapped ever so lightly at my door.

'Yes?' I called.

Leland put his head in. 'I just wanted to say good night,' he said.

'Good night, Leland.' I returned his smile.

'Now you get right into bed, young lady. And don't have any bad dreams. That's an order.'

The door closed quietly. Leland's footsteps receded across the hall. I frowned after him. Was he checking on me? Why were they both making such a point about my getting to bed so early? It was barely nine o'clock. Or was I being overly suspicious?

I turned out the light and began undressing in the moonlight that streamed through the window, though I had no intention of going to sleep. I lay there staring up at the ceiling. Yet despite my staunch intentions to stay awake, I found myself getting drowsy.

I couldn't be sure whether it had been a flash of lightning or a clap of thunder that woke me later. I stirred in my bed, slowly opening my eyes, becoming aware of the sound of raindrops. I'd never heard such rain. It didn't seem to blow or sweep, it sounded as if it were falling straight down, unhindered by wind or gale. The drops were huge and splattering.

I sat up in bed to watch the rivulets of water as they streamed down the window panes. After a few minutes, I got up and went back to the window seat, wrapping myself in my housecoat, and raised the window an inch or so to let in the delicious smell of night flowers, vivid and freshly awakened by the sudden rain.

Below my window, at the edge of the tree line, something moved. I eased the window up higher and leaned out, feeling the droplets of rain on my face and hair. My eyes widened. Far below me stood Diana and Leland, both clad in rain hats and slickers. Leland carried a large burlap sack. They whispered together for a moment, and disappeared into the woods.

What in the world were Diana and Leland doing tramping around in the woods in this downpour? It made no sense.

A sudden thought filtered through my sleep-laden brain. Leland and Diana were outside. Other than Hattie and Martin, I was alone in Falcon House. Perhaps now was as good a chance as any to do some investigating.

I slipped my feet into soft slippers and went quietly across the little room, easing open the door, and stepped out into the hall. Even though the hour was late and I was tired, my senses seemed to be overly keen. I went slowly past the closed doors that lined the corridor. I purposely hadn't taken my crutch, so my progress was slow.

It occurred to me, if they meant to hide

anything from me here in this house they would not have housed that mystery in this wing. I'd have to find access to the south end of the mansion.

I went past the door to the private elevator and found myself on a gallery overlooking the huge entrance hall. The weirdly patterned staircase lay at my feet. A single light shone below, just inside the front door. I listened for a moment to the sound of the rain on the shingled roof. How long Diana and Leland would be wandering around outside I didn't know. My search would have to be done hastily and in stages.

I crossed the gallery and came to a pair of massive double doors. Surprisingly, the doors eased open with only a feeble groan. I found myself in a darkened passageway. Other passageways went off to left and right, with many doors, some open, some closed. As I passed the open doors I tried to look into those rooms but they were too dark to really see anything. The main passage took several angled turns through this labyrinth. Then suddenly the hallway came to an abrupt end.

A second set of double doors blocked my way. These doors were a little more difficult to open. I had to put my shoulder to them and lever myself against the cast on my leg.

Another corridor. More doors. I heard scurrying and fluttering and knew that my only companions in this wing of the sagging old mansion were bats and spiders and mice. The thought made my flesh crawl. A heavy dead silence lay over everything.

Go back, a tiny voice said, but I shook my head slowly. No, I had to find out. I had to know, regardless of the price. I screwed up my waning courage and pushed on down the corridor. I felt like a fly fighting its way across a thick, molding cobweb, waiting for the marauding spider to pounce any second.

I saw a chink of light under a door at the far end of the hallway. It was only the dimmest sliver of light, but it looked to me like a beacon in comparison to the dreary darkness that surrounded me on all sides.

I hurried toward it. When I laid my

hand on the doorknob I noticed that it was smooth and clean to the touch. I turned the knob slowly. The door swung back noiselessly. As I entered the room beyond my eyes got wider and wider. Before me gleamed a brightly lighted wall of glass bricks. The glass wall ran from floor to ceiling, like a shimmering cascade of frozen water. A solid door, vented at the bottom, was the only break in the gleaming glass barrier. Slowly I went toward it.

'Who's there?' I heard a young, feminine voice ask. 'Who's there?'

I swallowed hard. I'd found what I'd been searching for. I heard her jiggle the knob. The door was locked.

I stood frozen in my tracks.

6

'Daddy, is that you?' the voice on the other side of the door asked.

I didn't move. I couldn't. I'd found what I'd been hoping to find. I was close to the solution to the puzzle, yet I found myself shaking inside.

'I know someone's out there,' she said, sounding annoyed. 'Don't play games with me. Martin, is that you? I can hear you breathing.'

I went slowly toward the door and pressed my ear tight against the solid panel.

'It's Alice Whelan,' I said softly. My voice seemed to boom out through the emptiness of the place.

I thought I heard a sharp intake of breath. 'Alice Whelan? Who's Alice Whelan?'

'I'm visiting here,' I told her. 'I'm Diana Hamilton's daughter.'

'Diana Hamilton? Oh, yes, my stepmother.' She laughed softly. 'They didn't tell you that you had a stepsister, did they? How did you know I was here?'

'I saw the light under the door. I was just roaming about. I couldn't sleep. Are you locked in?'

'What a silly question. Of course I'm locked in. You don't think I'd stay in here of my own choice, do you?'

'Why? Why do they keep you locked up in there?'

'Because I'll run away,' she answered, sounding embittered.

'Why?'

'Why, why, why,' she said impatiently. 'Wouldn't you run away if your father kept you locked up in this horrible old place? I run away every chance I get.'

It had to be the same girl I'd seen this morning. 'What's your name? Why are you in there?'

'I'm Sarah. This is where I live.'

'Sarah?'

'Sarah Braddock, of course. Oh, are you dumb.' She sounded more impatient than ever.

'I don't understand. Why does your father keep you locked up? Aren't you ever allowed out?'

'Only when I get a chance to pick the lock. I'm very good at picking locks,' she added, laughing gaily.

'Did you pick this lock this morning?'

'This morning? Yes, I think it was this morning.'

'And you got to Gulf Point before Martin caught up with you?'

'Yes, that's right. But how did you know?'

'I saw you,' I said, sounding breathless. 'You were running away from Martin.'

'But where did you see me? Where were you?'

'On the train as it was pulling into Gulf Point station. I saw you from the window of my compartment. I saw Martin strike you and put you in the car.' I found my voice was trembling. 'I tried to report it, but everyone said I imagined it all.'

'They would,' Sarah said in a dismissive tone. 'They don't want anyone to know about me. You mustn't tell them you found me. They wouldn't like that a bit. Promise me you won't tell. Promise me. Oh, please, promise.'

'Yes, I promise,' I found myself saying. 'Don't worry. I won't tell anyone.'

I heard her sigh with relief. 'Good. It'll be our secret for now — and you'll help me to escape, won't you, Alice Whelan?'

I didn't know what to say.

'Are you still there?' she asked after a moment of silence.

'Yes, I'm still here.' I hesitated. 'Why are you kept locked in this room?'

'My father doesn't want me to go out into the outside world.'

'But why?'

'You don't know my father. Just because he isn't happy on the outside, he wants to protect me. He keeps me a prisoner. He doesn't want anybody out there to hurt me.'

'But that doesn't make any sense,' I told her.

'You must believe me. My father was once a very famous scientist. He did a lot of research with plants and flowers. He found some kind of plant secretion that would keep people from getting old. He told the people at the Institute about it and they laughed at him. And now he doesn't want to have anything to do with those people outside and he doesn't want them to get a chance to hurt me.'

'But that's utterly ridiculous.' I suddenly found myself seething with anger at Leland Braddock. What right did he have to punish a young girl simply because of his own unhappy experience?

Sarah groaned. 'You mustn't tell. You mustn't let him know you know I'm here. Daddy would only hide me someplace else if you told him.'

'I won't tell him, Sarah.'

'And you'll help me get away from here?'

'Yes. I'll do what I can.' I didn't know exactly what that would be, but I knew I had to do something.

'I can pick this lock easily,' Sarah said from the other side of the door. 'I only need a little more time to fool with it. My biggest problem is getting across the gulf. I don't know how to operate any of the motorboats. I used a rowboat this morning, but Martin found me gone and took off after me. He's so cruel when he catches me. But if you help, I could get away.'

'What can I do?'

'If you said you wanted to borrow the boat, I could slip into it and hide. Once we got to the other side it would be easy for me to get away.'

'But where would you go? How would you manage? Surely you're not old enough to fend for yourself.'

'I'm eighteen,' she said defiantly.

I envisioned the little girl racing across the field again. She'd seemed barely in her teens, but I'd been a distance away.

I found myself frowning. 'And you've been kept in there all these years?'

'Yes, for most of them. I was quite young when father had all that trouble at the Institute.'

'How terrible. But what of your schooling?'

'They bring me books and stuff,' she answered offhandedly. 'I don't like school anyway.'

'But you can't just run out into the world. You must . . . '

A noise, soft and far away suddenly cut

me off. I cocked my ear toward the corridor. I heard the shuffle of footsteps. 'Someone's coming,' I whispered hurriedly.

'Get out of here,' Sarah whispered back. 'They mustn't find you. It'll spoil everything if they find you.'

'I'll come again tomorrow.' The noises got closer and closer.

'Get Martin or somebody to show you how to drive the motorboats. Get used to borrowing them so that we can make our escape,' she said hurriedly. 'I've rowed across before, but it takes too long.'

I noticed that she was using the plural noun, we. Yes, of course; that would be the solution. I'd help her get away and take her with me back to Hillsborough. That would be the only way. I'd get her away from this awful place and its awful people. I'd go to the law, if I had to, in order to protect Sarah against her father.

The footsteps got louder. 'Good night, Sarah,' I whispered.

'Take the corridor to the left,' she said. 'Go down the back way. They won't see you if you hurry.'

I turned back toward the corridor. There was a light coming along the hallway. I went to the left — away from it — and tried to move quickly and silently in spite of the heavy cast on my leg. I hid myself around the corner, pressing myself flat against the wall, and held my breath. I didn't dare peek around to see who was coming toward Sarah's solarium. Whoever it was wasn't talking. I heard what sounded like the growls of an animal.

'I'll hold that,' Leland's voice said. 'You get the door.'

I heard him call his daughter's name. Thinking it was surely not wise to remain where I was, I slid along the wall, being careful not to thump my cast against anything. After I moved out of hearing distance I went as quickly as I could down to the end of the corridor and found the back stairs.

A door at the bottom opened onto a pantry. The hinges creaked as I inched the door open, and I froze. After a moment, I carefully peeked around it. The room, what I could see of it in the dim light, was empty. I crept out of the back stairway and crossed the room as noiselessly as possible. My feet felt chilled, and my broken leg ached as I made my way toward another door.

It opened onto the dining room. The rain had stopped and the moonlight from outside showed my way clearly. I skirted the massive table and chairs and went toward the entrance hall.

'Who's there?' I heard someone call.

Quickly I crouched down behind one of the chairs just as the pantry door swung open. From my hiding place I saw Martin's face illuminated in the beam of his flashlight. I crawled underneath the dining table and felt sure he could hear the pounding of my heart as well as the thump of my cast against the rug.

The beam of his light flashed across the room, moving slowly from corner to corner. I saw his feet move past me as he went toward the hall.

'Is someone there?' he asked again, moving out into the entrance hall. I saw the light shift from right to left, up and down, back and forth. I kept still and tried not to breathe.

How long I stayed crouched under that table, I couldn't be sure. It seemed like hours. My knees felt sore and my cast felt heavier than ever as I knelt under the table. In spite of the chill of the room I could feel beads of perspiration on my brow.

After what seemed an eternity, the beam of the flashlight came back into the dining room. Martin's feet passed the table. I felt a sudden tickle in my throat. Oh no, I prayed. I couldn't cough. I tightened my throat against the urge. My throat tickled and throbbed. I tried to swallow. I couldn't. Martin went back into the pantry and the door swung shut after him. I breathed a sigh of relief and found that the tickle in my throat was gone.

I lost no time getting out from my hiding place. I was careful not to disturb the position of the chairs as I crept out, dragging the cast behind me, then hurried out into the entrance hall. I limped across the floor and up the patchwork staircase. As I made my way up the first flight I realized that if someone — anyone

— came into the hall or out onto the gallery, I would certainly be spotted. There was no place to hide.

The insane staircase seemed to have no end. My feet were icy cold. My leg was throbbing unmercifully under the plaster cast. My breathing was labored. I was sure I'd never reach the top. My head started to pound as I mounted the last steps.

The gallery rail was just at eye level. I looked in both directions to make sure the way was clear. Slowly I eased myself up the last few steps and stepped onto the gallery floor. The corridor was empty.

Then I heard Diana and Leland coming from the opposite direction. They'd obviously finished their visit to Sarah and would be coming back to their room — the room directly across the hall from my own.

Would I make it in time? I tried to judge their distance by the sound of their muffled voices. I'd have to chance it, I told myself. I had no other choice. If they found me at the top of the stairway, standing on the gallery, they'd know that

I'd been nosing about.

Hobbling as fast as I could down the corridor, I reached the door of my room just as I heard the door at the far end of the corridor swing open. I rushed into my room and flattened myself against the back of the door.

I was panting heavily, my face streaked with sweat. The pounding in my head was excruciating. I stood motionless, listening as Diana and Leland came down the hall. If they tried the door to my room and found me pressed against it, they'd easily guess what I'd been up to. One look at me would tell them all they had to know. Yet I was fearful they'd hear the thumping of my leg cast if I started across my room now. I stood there, praying they'd go directly into their room.

My luck held. I heard their door open and close. Quickly I went toward the bed, shaking off my housecoat and slippers as I went. I threw myself down and shut my eyes. I felt the stinging behind my lids. I bit into the back of my hand just as I heard the door across the hall open again.

I threw my arm across my eyes and

pulled the covers up around my neck. The door to my room opened a few inches. I heard someone come into the room and I smelled Diana's perfume. She was standing over me. I kept my eyes tightly shut and held myself in check.

Finally she turned and left.

'Oh, my God,' I breathed softly as the door closed after her. The tears came easily and quickly. I threw myself face down on the pillows and gave myself up to them.

I kept telling myself I mustn't cry. I must think. I must plan. Stop crying, Alice. Stop crying.

I cried myself to sleep.

7

The morning broke so bright and clear it was difficult to imagine the storm I'd seen the night before. I couldn't remember falling asleep after Diana left my room. The brightness and clearness of the day made my thoughts just as bright and clear and I wanted them to stay that way.

I'd go to Sarah as soon as an opportunity presented itself and I'd tell her I planned on going with her — away from this dreadful house and its people. I had no real reason to stay here. I shouldn't have come in the first place. I wasn't wanted. I wasn't loved, and I would not be missed.

I threw back the coverlet and swung my feet over the side of the bed. I'd have to make plans if I were to prepare a successful escape for Sarah and myself. Her suggestion was a good one, that I begin with the speedboats. I'd invent excuses for using them and let Diana and

Leland accustom themselves to seeing me driving off over the gulf.

I remembered that Justin was coming this morning and that thought made the morning brighter still. I wondered if he knew about Sarah. He must know. Leland hardly could have kept her secret from his own brother. His slip at the lunch table yesterday, his guilty look convinced me that Justin knew.

I'd have to play that by ear. Surely he didn't condone his brother's actions in keeping the girl locked away like some wild beast.

And what had Diana and Leland been doing in the woods in last night's downpour? What had they been toting when they went to Sarah's solarium? I remembered the low, animal growls I'd heard in the corridor and shivered.

Would Justin help if I told him of my plot? I asked myself that very same question as I sat alone at the breakfast table on the terrace watching Justin tie up his boat and start toward the house with a small overnight bag in his hand.

'Hello there,' he greeted me as he came

onto the terrace. 'You look as beautiful as the day.'

I flushed slightly. 'Flattery will get you everywhere,' I told him, returning his brilliant smile. 'Coffee?'

'Yes, please,' he said, seating himself across from me. 'Where are the landlords? Still in bed?'

'I suppose. I haven't seen anyone except Hattie.'

He stretched and reached for the coffee cup I set in front of him. 'I never was one for sleeping late, I'm afraid.' When I raised my eyes I found him smiling at me.

'You do look like Diana,' he commented. There was a definite touch of appreciation in his voice which made me flush all the more.

'Thank you.'

He eyed me over the rim of his cup. 'Tell me about yourself.'

I had my elbows propped on the table, and was cradling my coffee cup. 'There's not much to tell if you've read the newspaper accounts,' I told him.

He kept his eyes fixed on me. 'For

some reason or other I just couldn't bring myself to believing that 'long lost daughter' routine.'

My coffee cup clanged against the saucer. I looked at him with surprise.

'Aha,' he said, grinning like the Cheshire cat. 'I knew I was right.'

I tried to look composed and not show that he'd caught me off guard. No one disbelieved Diana's story. Why had Justin? The fact that he did pleased me immensely. 'What makes you think you're right in not believing the newspapers?' I asked, trying to sound casual and matter-of-fact.

'I know the great Diana Hamilton. I met her before Leland — in fact, I introduced them. Diana loves to make a melodrama out of everything.'

'You introduced Diana to Leland?' I tried to veer the subject away from me.

He nodded. 'I was surprised, however, when Leland told me they were going to marry. The Diana Hamilton I met always preferred younger men, or didn't you know that?' He said it without malice, without any insulting innuendo. I myself had wondered, when I saw Leland, why Diana had chosen him. It *was* a known fact that Diana's husbands had all been much, much younger than herself — until Leland, of course. For my mother's sake, I tried to look shocked.

'That isn't very kind,' I admonished lightly.

He kept his eyes on mine. 'Are you really her daughter?'

'Yes, I am.'

'Her 'long lost daughter'?'

I found myself smiling. 'No, not really,' I said truthfully. 'Diana has always known where to reach me if she wanted to.'

'I thought as much.' He leaned across the table and took my hand. 'And I can understand why she wanted to keep you in the background. You're very lovely, you know.'

I felt the electric shock again and withdrew my hand as tactfully as I could. I was blushing like a schoolgirl.

'So you'd met Diana before Leland?' I said, changing the subject away from me again.

He leaned back in his chair, dropping

one arm over the back. 'Yes, I met her in a nightclub.'

'A nightclub. You hardly look the type,' I said.

He merely laughed. 'Well, behind this bookish exterior lies a dissolute soul.' He gave a careless wave of his hand. 'I enjoy nightclubs occasionally. I like fun and gaiety spliced into my mundane life. It's a nice change of pace. Don't you agree?'

'A necessary change of pace, I think. All work and no play, et cetera.'

'And what do you do when you close down the classroom and send the little beggars off for home?'

'I don't go to nightclubs. Not that there's anything wrong with them, but for a single girl alone it isn't considered respectable. How did you happen to meet my mo . . . Diana — in a nightclub?'

He shrugged. 'I was having a drink at the bar and enjoying the show. She was coming out of the powder room and jostled into me. We got to talking. She invited me to her table. It was as simple as that.'

'Just like that,' I said. 'And do you

make a habit of going around letting older women pick you up?'

He laughed. 'I'm a fan of Diana's. I always have been. I was flattered. She was charming. Now don't let that devious little mind of yours start making mountains out of mole hills. I merely had a drink with the lady and her friends.'

'And you never saw her again?'

'Of course I saw her again. She called me at school the next afternoon.'

'She called *you?*' I said, truly shocked.

'What's wrong with that?' he asked. 'It's done every day, or didn't you know?'

'I wasn't exactly raised in a convent.' For some reason the whole story of his encounter with my mother sounded sordid and seedy and I didn't really want to hear any more of it. 'But she is my mother, after all.'

'Oh, you are the prim and proper little one, aren't you? We'll have to do something about that.'

I put my cup down with a gesture of finality. 'I really should be going in,' I said, at a loss for something better to say.

He gave me a strange, dumbfounded

look. 'Going in where?'

I fumbled uncomfortably with my chair. 'I have a few letters to write,' I lied. 'I've neglected them too long.'

'Am I frightening you away? I didn't want to do that,' he said. 'I'm sorry.'

I felt so uncomfortable. 'There's nothing to apologize for.'

'Yes, there is,' he said, reaching again for my hand. His grip was hard and strong. 'I've given you a very bad impression of both your mother and myself, and especially of your mother. That was not very nice of me. I apologize.'

'My mother's reputation is well known,' I said, trying to sound grown-up. 'She wouldn't appreciate your apologizing for her.'

'Whether Diana called me or didn't call me is immaterial. The important thing is that I introduced her to my brother, Leland. They fell in love. I think that's wonderful, don't you?'

'I suppose,' I said, again barely hearing myself. All I could think about was how wonderful my hand felt in his.

Martin suddenly appeared in the doorway. Instantly I withdrew my hand from Justin's. Martin stood for a moment watching us ... me in particular. Suddenly the memory of last night rushed back at me.

'I'd like to go for a boat ride,' I said brightly. 'Justin? Could you show me how to drive?'

'What about your letters?'

'Oh, they've waited this long, they can wait a couple more hours.'

'All right then, a boat ride it is,' he said, getting to his feet. 'Come along, Miss Whelan, I will give you your first lesson in navigation.'

Justin linked my arm in his and I leaned on him as we made our way down toward the jetty. The day was indeed beautiful; more beautiful than when I'd awakened. The sea was like glass, the sky clear and blue. There seemed to be no air stirring.

Justin helped me into the boat, untied the line and got in beside me. 'This is the ignition switch,' he said. 'Just like a car's.' He reached for a little knob and pulled it out. 'This is the choke.' He twisted the ignition key. The boat roared to life. 'See, it's as simple as that.' He showed me how to manipulate the gears, how to back up, how to increase and decrease speed. It was all so simple a child could do it.

When Justin let me take the wheel I found I had a tendency of cutting too sharply on my turns, making the boat tip dangerously to right and left. Justin showed me how to turn the wheel slowly so that the boat moved more gracefully around curves. I liked having him close to me, his hands over mine.

Then he got behind the wheel again and opened up the throttle. He sped along at a hellish clip, sending the water streaming out behind us. He spun and curved and dipped and splashed through our own wake. It was fun, even though I knew I looked a little ridiculous in the bright orange life jacket he made me put on. I hated for the ride to end.

'All right, now you take her in,' he said as he relinquished the controls back to me.

I did an almost expert job.

'You'll make a good sailor,' he complimented as he again helped me out of the boat and we started back toward Falcon House. We both happened to look up at the glass solarium at the same time. Sarah darted away from the window.

I stopped dead in my tracks.

'What is it?' Justin asked. He looked sheepish. He'd seen her too. He knew.

'I know about Sarah,' I told him, keeping my voice low. 'I talked to her.'

He grabbed my arm so hard he hurt me slightly. He spun me toward him. 'You must never do that, Alice. Promise me. Stay away from Sarah. You mustn't go near her.'

'So you're in on her being kept prisoner here too?'

'You don't understand.' His face was dark and serious. 'Sarah is a very dangerous young lady. You must not go near her again, do you understand?' The fingers of his hands were digging into my flesh.

I cringed away from him. 'How could you condone Leland's barbarous actions? That girl is a prisoner here. And you let him keep her one.'

'Don't be a fool,' he said in a low, rasping voice. 'Don't go near Sarah again. Promise me. And for God's sake, Alice, don't tell anybody else that you know Sarah's in that old solarium.'

'Why? Why is Sarah kept up there?'

He looked away from me. 'I can't tell you that. Not here — not now.'

Diana's voice called down to us from the terrace. She waved and started toward us.

'Just keep quiet about what you know,' Justin whispered urgently. 'I'll explain it all later.'

Diana, in her usual grand manner, descended upon us.

8

Diana held court all day long. She insisted we go over to the mainland for a late lunch, something that surprised Leland greatly. Diana never left Falcon Island, it seemed. But she was in gay spirits and it was difficult not to let myself get swept up into her good mood. The day passed most enjoyably, even if I couldn't really appreciate it. My mind was too taken up with thoughts of Sarah and what Justin wanted to tell me about her.

Justin was most attentive to me; unfortunately we didn't find a single moment alone in which to pursue our discussion of Sarah.

Gulf Point was far from being a thriving metropolis, yet it was an enchanting little town with good restaurants, charming shops and an old world feeling. It had an atmosphere of friendly warmth that radiated from its inhabitants and captivated its visitors.

The afternoon was a pleasant one for all of us. Even Leland seemed more relaxed than I'd thought him capable of being. Of course, it was difficult to remain unaffected by Diana's exuberance. For one entire afternoon she was the mother I'd always dreamed she'd be, charming, witty, thoughtful — almost loving.

She doted on Leland. And all the previous notions Justin had caused me to conjure up about her vanished. I suppose I'd been looking for reasons to dislike her when Justin spoke of the nightclub incident and her telephoning him. I wanted to think of her as an immoral woman, a Jezebel. I was being horribly old-fashioned and unfair and I knew it.

We started back to Falcon Island late in the afternoon. I shivered slightly as we again drove into that dreary rain forest that skirted the gulf.

'It is rather a dreadful old place, isn't it, Alice?' Diana said.

Justin laughed softly. 'You ladies have

no true appreciation of the beauties of nature. That rain forest is a treasure.'

Justin helped me into the boat. I was pleased and flattered when Diana reached for my hand and seated me beside her. It was the first time she'd shown any interest in the problems my leg cast created for me.

'That thing must be horribly uncomfortable,' she said. 'I wish you didn't have to wear it.'

'It just itches,' I told her with a broad smile.

'That isn't very glamorous,' she said, matching my smile. 'And ladies should always be glamorous.'

Leland steered the boat toward Falcon Island. 'Were you glamorous in your leg cast, my dear?'

'Of course,' she answered with a flippant wave of her hand. 'I had my make-up man gild it for me.'

I laughed in spite of myself.

Once we were back inside Falcon House, however, Diana's mood suddenly became dark. Justin insisted that cocktails be served in the lovely bright drawing room, but even the beauty of that room didn't do anything to bring Diana's spirits back up to their afternoon level. She sat quietly next to Leland and toyed with the stem of her glass.

Through dinner she merely picked at her food and only answered questions asked her. The change was uncanny, unnerving. It seemed as though the house exuded some kind of spell over her. Even Justin was incapable of bringing her out of her depression.

'I'm being a terrible bore this evening,' she said as we decided to have coffee and a liqueur in the drawing room. 'I'm going to bed if no one objects,' she announced.

'But it's so early,' Leland said.

I saw her smile faintly. 'I'm tired. It's been a long afternoon.'

Leland got up when she did.

'No, no,' Diana said, waving him back into his chair. 'You stay and keep the children entertained, darling. I'll see you all in the morning.'

I had half hoped that they'd leave Justin and me to ourselves so that I could get to the bottom of the Sarah mystery. Unfortunately Leland resumed his seat, settling himself into a conversation with his brother about Justin's work at the college.

'I don't think we should bore Alice with lab talk,' Justin said. 'My projects are all coming along very well. I'll tell you about them tomorrow,' he said to his brother.

Again I sensed that there was some sort of message passing between them, but I had no idea what it was. I thought I should try to find out. 'What projects are you working on?' I asked Justin.

He shrugged indifferently. 'Nothing very exciting, I'm afraid. Leland got me hooked on botany. I work with plant life.'

I suddenly remembered Sarah's talk about Leland's theory of counteracting the aging process in humans through the use of plant secretions. Was Justin pursuing such a project? I wondered.

Leland leaned toward me. 'We Braddocks have always been very interested in plant life. Do you know anything about botany, Alice?'

'Only what they taught me in college,

I'm afraid, which wasn't very much.'

'Are you interested?'

My thoughts flew to Sarah. 'I suppose so, yes. At least I love flowers.'

Leland slapped his knee and got up. 'Well then, Justin, how about you and me showing Alice our pride and joy.'

I gave him a vacant look.

Justin got out of his chair. 'We have one of the most unique greenhouses in the country,' he said. 'Do you feel up to taking a little tour?'

'The solarium?' I asked. My voice felt tight and I could feel my insides beginning to shake. Would they dare take me to Sarah and her prison?

Leland chuckled. 'No, not the old solarium. I'm afraid that outlived its usefulness a long, long time ago. No, we had a greenhouse built at the rear of the property. It isn't far and it is really quite educational.'

'I'd love to see it,' I said, feeling slightly disappointed.

I limped between them out through the back end of the house. Hattie was at the sink when we went through the kitchen.

Martin was sitting at a table sipping coffee. His eyes followed us across the room. I could feel them boring into my back as we let ourselves out the back door.

The greenhouse was a low slung building settled in the center of a clearing. Its square glass panes and tilted roof made it look like a cut gem glimmering in the moonlight. Dim lights shone dully through the frosted windows.

Once inside the glass building the atmosphere closed in like a dense fog. My breath came with more effort as I stood surveying the rows upon rows of growth, some potted, some in flats, some climbing both vertically as well as horizontally. It was a wonderland of color and scent, yet it reminded me of the dreary rain forest at the edge of the mainland and I felt sweaty and uncomfortable. Justin took my elbow and led me toward a row of blossoming flowers that winked and bobbed under an overhead lamp.

'I don't want to shock you, Alice,' Leland said, 'but I must warn you not to touch any of these beauties. Almost every species of plant growing here is *insectivorous*.'

'Carnivorous, he means,' Justin explained. 'But they're quite harmless if you leave them alone.'

'They give me the willies just looking at them,' I stammered, averting my eyes from the moss-like growth that I'd almost touched.

'Now, now,' Leland admonished. 'You mustn't close your eyes to the wonders of nature. Everything has its place in this beautiful world of ours.' He hesitated, as though reflecting, then added, 'Well, almost everything.'

I didn't want to stay in that hot, muggy place. I wanted to go back out into the fresh air — even back to Falcon House. The atmosphere of Falcon House was depressing, to say the least, but it didn't have half the ugly morbidity that this place radiated.

Leland touched my arm. 'Remember, my dear,' he started, 'on the whole, the animal world preys on the vegetable world, so isn't it only fair that for a change the vegetable gets a chance at the animal?'

The thought was gruesome, but I didn't tell him so.

'Now this is what is called a small Liverwort,' Justin explained, stopping alongside a bin with little red plants skimming its surface.

'The *Frullanian tamarisci*,' Leland announced. 'It grows on the bark of trees normally but we've improved the species, I think, by implanting it in the earth where it has access to more abundant meals.'

Justin picked up a small stick and lifted the moss-like growth. 'See, here beneath its ordinary leaves it has small sack-like leaves which are used to catch its prey.'

Leland again touched my arm and led me on. 'It is among the higher flowering plants that one finds the most extraordinary and purposeful arrangements for capturing and digesting prey,' he said.

'Take this one, for instance.' He pointed to a huge flower which appeared to have no stems. Its odor was obnoxious.

'The *Dischidia Rafflesiana*. It's a curious plant in which the leaves have become quite like a pitcher, or a flower pot, if you prefer. It holds rain and leaf mould in its little container. It uses rain water in which to drown its prey.'

I felt my head swim and turned abruptly away. I wanted to get away from the animal-eating growths. I purposely walked toward some hanging vines. 'I hope this isn't carnivorous,' I said, studying the vine.

Leland and Justin walked over to where I went to stand. 'No,' Leland explained, 'on this side of the greenhouse we keep the vegetarians.'

I shot him a look. Justin merely grinned.

'I call them vegetarians,' Leland explained, 'because they live on other plants. They're parasites. Many flowering plants, including mistletoe and dodder, have become parasitic. They fix themselves onto other plants and steal their food away from them. This vine, for instance, is what is called a *Stranglerfig*, which lives in tropical places. They climb to the tops of trees. Then they send down root stems that grow tightly around the trunks of the trees and choke them. After the tree is dead and decayed, the stranglerfig remains erect, occupying the position of the tree it murdered.'

I grimaced.

'Now here are some white Indian pipes,' Leland went on. 'These, together with their cousin the blood-red snow plants, are *saprophytic*. They live on the dead and decaying vegetable matter in forests.'

'Horrible,' I gasped, turning away.

'Not at all. It's all part of living,' Leland said casually.

I swallowed hard. 'I don't really think I'm up to all this,' I managed to say. 'It's a bit gruesome, I think.'

Justin turned me back toward the carnivorous plants. 'Leland and I have lived with these lovely old monsters all our lives. I guess we're hardened to the effect they have on some people.'

Leland moved ahead of us along the aisle. Once out of earshot Justin moved close to me. 'Try to stick it out, Alice,' he said. 'It will help me explain a lot about young Sarah.'

Leland turned to be sure we hadn't abandoned him. He motioned us toward him. Justin had said the magic word, 'Sarah.' I picked up my courage and went to where Leland was standing.

Suddenly a blaze of color caught my eyes. There was a long, wide stretch of lovely reddish rosettes of small rounded or spoon-shaped leaves lying on a field of mossy ground.

'Oh, how very beautiful,' I gushed, moving quickly toward the enchanting sight.

Leland grabbed my arm so hard and so fast I thought he'd wrenched my shoulder from its socket. I toppled backward against Justin, who slipped his arm around me and pulled me toward him.

'Don't go near that,' Justin whispered harshly.

The look on Leland's face was one of utter horror. Sweat was beading his brow. He took out a handkerchief and blotted his forehead.

'What's the matter?' I asked.

Leland was fighting to regain his composure. 'That's the Sundew,' he explained breathing hard. 'It's an extremely dangerous plant. I suppose its beauty is one of the reasons it's so lethal.'

He was still panting noticeably, although it was obvious that he was trying to calm himself. 'Each one of those leaves, as you can see, is covered by hundreds of glittering little dewdrops. The tentacles which cover the leaf secrete this glistening, sticky dew and there are hundreds upon hundreds of them on every single, solitary leaf. When anything alights on those conspicuous glittering, reddish leaves, it finds itself instantly trapped. But it isn't only the dew that entraps them; that's only a means for holding the insect fast. All the neighboring tentacles, although they have not been touched by the weight of the prey, bend over toward the victim and pin it down.'

He was still sweating profusely. I thought he looked as if he might become violently ill at any moment.

'Are you all right, Leland?' his brother asked.

'Yes, yes, fine, thank you. It's just . . . '

'I know,' Justin said, touching his brother's shoulder. 'Perhaps we should go back.'

Leland stood staring at the bed of Sundew flowers. He looked as though his eyes were glued to them and would remain glued to them forever — forever trapped by those glistening, shimmering leaves that waited to fold over him.

I felt Justin touch my arm. When I glanced at him, his eyes moved down to a printed sign at the front of the bed of Sundew flowers. One word was printed on it: DROSERA.

It made no sense. I frowned and looked up at Justin. He was studying me intently. He too wore a frown on his brow. He nodded again toward the sign and moved his lips, silently mouthing the word.

Drosera.

It still made no sense. I repeated the word slowly to myself. Why was Justin making such an obvious point of showing me a sign that bore a plant's name? Why didn't he just come right out and say the word? Why was he mouthing it; making such a big secret of it?

Dros . . . My mind suddenly clicked. It was the last syllable that made me gasp. Sera. Sarah. My eyes widened. I stared up at him.

Justin merely nodded.

9

I sat in my room reading, wondering if I would have a chance to see Justin before the night ended. My curiosity was so aroused I could hardly contain myself. What possible connection could there be between those awful carnivorous plants and young Sarah Braddock? It had to do with the Drosera flowers. Justin had made that quite clear. And Leland? How strangely he'd behaved when I went toward the Drosera. He was so stricken by the incident that he actually turned white.

I slammed the book shut and put it on the nightstand. Almost simultaneous with the noise of my book closing was the sound of a door across the hall opening and shutting. Seconds later there was a tap on my door.

'Yes?'

Diana put her head in. 'Not sleepy?' she asked.

'I was just turning in,' I told her. 'Are you feeling any better?'

She gave a little shrug of unconcern. 'Oh, I'm all right. The afternoon was just a bit busier than I'm generally accustomed to. A good night's sleep will put me back in my old form.' She was smiling, but it was forced. There was a darkness in her eyes that I'd noticed before. She was worried about something.

She didn't come into the room. All I could see of her was her head. 'Get some sleep, Alice. Did you drink the milk I had sent up?'

I glanced at the glass of milk on the nightstand. 'I'd almost forgotten about it,' I told her. 'But I don't think I'll need it to relax me. I'm really quite tired.'

'Drink it anyway. It's good for you.'

I didn't feel like arguing. 'I will,' I said.

'Good night, Alice, dear. I'll see you in the morning.'

'Good night,' I answered, absentmindedly reaching for the glass of milk. I picked it up just as the door closed.

The milk was sour tasting. I made a

face, got out of bed and poured it down the sink in the bathroom. I didn't really need anything to make me sleep. On the contrary, I wanted to stay awake and see if I couldn't find Justin. I simply couldn't go to sleep without talking to him about Sarah.

I slipped into my robe and went out into the hall and along the corridor. Diana's door was closed but I saw a sliver of light underneath. They weren't in bed as yet. I made a mental note of that and reminded myself I'd have to be as quiet as possible.

Luckily Justin's room was far down the corridor, almost at the end. When I reached it my heart sank a little. The door was open; the room was empty.

'Justin?' I said in a half whisper. I poked my head inside and looked around. Justin wasn't there.

Perhaps he had anticipated my wanting to talk to him and was waiting down-stairs. I turned and tried to hurry my steps. Just as I reached the elevator, walking carefully so that my leg cast wouldn't thud too loudly, I thought I saw the doors leading to the south wing move slightly.

I went to the doors. The moment I pushed them open I was sure I heard scurrying footsteps, light and swift receding into the darkness. I stood there in the dim light, listening.

I suddenly heard voices coming from the gallery I'd just crossed. I flattened myself against the wall, half expecting the double doors to be pushed open. Beads of perspiration began to form on my brow. What would be my excuse if Diana and Justin found me standing here in the dark — here in the wing that housed Sarah and the solarium?

The voices faded. I inched open the door and saw Diana and Leland disappear down the crazy-quilt staircase. Again they were carrying a sack and again they were dressed for the out-of-doors.

Why hadn't they used the elevator? And where did they go each night? What was in the woods surrounding Falcon House?

I breathed an inward sigh of relief when I heard the front door open and close.

They were out of the house, and this time I had a fairly good idea just how long they'd be gone and that they'd more than likely come to the solarium on their return. I found myself moving a little more recklessly down the dark, dusty corridors, past the many doors. I knew where I was going now and lost little time getting there.

The light shone under the door, just as before, when I approached the tower that housed the solarium. It was just as I had seen it last night, but with one very important difference. When I opened the outer door and found myself face to face with the wall of glass brick, the door in the glass-brick wall was standing open.

'Sarah,' I called softly as I went toward it.

'Here,' I heard her timid little voice answer.

She was a handsome girl, more beautiful than I imagined. Her thick, black hair hung down almost to her waist. It was glossy and beautifully waved. She was curled up on a little bed tucked away in one corner. When she saw me her full, red lips curled into a pleasing smile and her dark eyes shimmered with happiness.

She didn't get up from the bed, but from where I stood I guessed her to be about my own height and well proportioned. She carried the Braddock family resemblance. I could see a bit of Justin in her features, and a great deal of Leland. Her mother had obviously been an extremely striking woman. Sarah was wearing a stylish dress and when I stepped into the room I saw a light coat and a small vanity case sitting beside the door.

'I thought you weren't coming. I stole a small suitcase from the box room,' she said, nodding toward the vanity case. 'I was going to leave without you. You see I've picked the lock again.' She looked me up and down. 'So you're Alice.'

I smiled at her. 'Yes, I'm Alice.' I glanced around. 'I thought perhaps Justin might be here.'

'Justin? Oh, yes, my Uncle Justin. No,' she said slowly in measured tones, 'Uncle Justin seldom comes here, except when . . . ' She let her sentence dangle.

'I have a plan,' I started as I stepped across the room and went nearer to her. I thought I saw her cringe back, but then she relaxed and leaned toward me. She kept the smile well fixed on her mouth.

'A plan?'

'Yes,' I said a little breathlessly. 'I had Justin show me how to operate the speedboat today.'

'I saw. I was watching you from the window.'

'It's easy, Sarah. All you have to do is turn the ignition key in the dashboard. That starts the motor. Then you just steer it as you would an automobile. The speed lever just pushes forward and back, depending upon how fast you want to go.'

I was talking in a rush, but I felt I had to tell her as much as I could before Diana and Leland returned from their prowl.

'I could most likely manage that alone,' she said. 'It doesn't sound difficult.'

'It isn't difficult.' I took a few steps closer to her. 'But you mustn't go alone. I've thought of something that will make everything all right.'

Her eyes were fixed on mine. They were so dark, so limpid and lovely I felt it hard to look away from her. They were like twin magnets drawing me closer and closer to her.

'We'll go together,' I said. 'You'll come back with me to Hillsborough.'

She kept smiling and staring at me. I took another step closer.

'Hillsborough?'

'Yes, it's in California. I teach school there.'

'Can we leave tonight?' She asked, holding my gaze fixed firmly on hers.

I faltered. Something strange was happening and I couldn't quite figure out what it was. I was beginning to feel weak, as though my legs were suddenly turning to gelatin. My body started to ache all over. I needed to sit down. I looked around for a chair. There was a small straight backed one against the wall. I went to it and pulled it up near Sarah on the bed. Once I sat down I felt a little better.

'Not tonight,' I told her, sensing the room come back into perspective. 'I can't leave tonight. I'm not ready. Besides, I need to . . . ' I intended to tell her I needed to talk to Justin but for some reason or other my words seemed to melt away into nothing. I was beginning to feel faint again.

'But I want to leave tonight,' she answered petulantly. 'I don't need your help now that I know about the boats.'

'Oh, but you do. Wait until tomorrow, Sarah. We'll steal away together. I can keep you with me in Hillsborough and see that you get the proper schooling. We'll work things out with your father once we're far away from him.'

Sarah suddenly laughed. She flipped her long dark hair back over her shoulders and leaned toward me, again capturing my eyes with hers. I couldn't look away from her. I tried to raise my hands and brush them across my face but they wouldn't obey me.

The cast on my leg suddenly seemed more leaden than ever. My body felt as though it weighed tons. I was sure the chair I sat in would collapse under my weight at any second.

What was happening to me?

'Sarah . . . ' I started, but my words were beginning to slur.

Again I heard her soft laugh, but it sounded so far, far away. I swayed in the chair, unable to focus. My head was swimming, my blood pulsed loudly through my veins.

The milk, I thought through the misty recesses of my mind. Had Diana put a drug of some kind in my milk?

I couldn't think anymore. The room was suddenly stiflingly hot. I tried to tug at the sash of my robe but again my hands and arms wouldn't cooperate. I couldn't move a single muscle. My head lolled to one side. My vision started to fade.

'I will leave tonight,' I heard Sarah say through the mist and the fog, the blackness that was sweeping over me.

I tried to say something but my voice wouldn't come. My lips barely moved. My mouth was dry as parched sand. I couldn't see. I tried desperately to move, to get out of the chair, but my own dead weight held me fast.

Far, far away I heard the creak of the bed. Sarah was getting up. I could feel the heat of her body as she moved toward me. Her hand on my forehead felt hot and clammy. I could feel her hot sweet breath on my face as she bent toward me.

'Alice,' I heard her say softly.

Help me, help me, my mind kept screaming, but my voice wouldn't put it into words. I was completely paralyzed. Somehow I managed to flutter open my eyes, but I saw nothing except a dim form looming over me.

'Alice,' she said again in that soft, velvety voice of hers.

I rolled my eyes and tried to tell her of my distress, but she seemed blind to everything. She merely soothed my brow and kept saying my name over and over and over.

I felt the pressure of her body leaning against mine as she helped me out of the chair and laid me on her bed. I was only barely conscious of anything. I knew where I was, but that was all I knew.

Again my eyelids fluttered. I focused

for a fraction of a second and saw her looking down at me. Then I felt the mattress sag as she leaned down over me.

My eyes drooped closed and a sudden terrifying pain ran through my body. The blackness swept over me.

10

'AAAAlllliiiiccccceeee.'

A flash, soundless but blinding, suddenly lighted up the black, but it was like the blink of lightning that warns of a raging storm.

'Allliiicccee.'

My mouth flew open but my scream was silent, dead. 'Alice.'

'Alice!'

Hands gripped my shoulders, shaking me, shaking me hard. The blackness seemed to turn to gray, to white, to light. My body was trembling, tears streaming down my cheeks. The hands gripping my shoulders loosened. The fingers relaxed and started to caress, sooth my trembling, aching body.

'Alice. Are you all right?'

I was afraid to open my eyes. I didn't want to know where I was. I was too afraid to face the possibility that I might be dead, lost, gone from the world forever.

'Alice. It's me, Justin. Are you all right?'

'Justin.' My eyes flew open. Justin leaned over me, handsome face creased with worry. I threw myself against him and buried my face against his chest. 'Oh, Justin,' I cried.

'There, there,' he said softly. 'You're all right now. Here, relax back against the pillows.' He held something to my lips. 'Drink this. It will help bring your strength back.'

My mind was still too dazed to know what I was doing. I drank deeply of whatever he offered me. It tasted thick and bitter but I drank it down, all of it.

I gave a deep sigh and lay back. 'What happened?' I asked dully, running my hand across my face. 'I don't remember. Where am I?'

'You're in your room. I carried you here. You'll be fine. Just rest. I'll stay with you until you're asleep.'

I turned my head and saw the closed door, the familiar room which Diana had assigned to me. 'No,' I said quickly. 'You mustn't stay here. Mother . . . '

'Hush. They don't know,' he said. 'And they mustn't know, Alice.'

'Know?' My mind wasn't functioning at full capacity as yet. 'Know what?'

'That I found you with Sarah.'

'But . . . ' I tried to sit up.

Justin eased me back against the pillows. 'Don't try to move or talk.'

I lay there fighting to focus my vision. I could see Justin, but his shape was frayed around the edges and he looked so far, far away. Unconsciously I reached out and touched him. I saw him smile as he took my hand.

'I'd explain,' he started, 'but I don't think you'd understand any of it right now. You need rest. You need to get your strength back.'

'But what happened to me?'

'It's Sarah.' he glanced anxiously toward the closed door. 'But I can't go into it now. Leland and Diana mustn't know I'm here with you, or that you found Sarah in the solarium.'

'Why not?'

'Because it would only upset them. It's better they don't know, at least not just yet.'

I felt the medicine he'd given me begin to put warmth back into my body. My mind was beginning to clear and my vision was beginning to sharpen.

'Poor, poor Sarah,' I moaned. 'Why, oh why do they treat her as they do? It's horrible to think they keep that child a prisoner.'

'They must. They have no other choice.'

'I don't understand.'

Justin hesitated. He continued to hold my hand in his. He leaned closer and said, 'Are you strong enough to listen if I explain?'

'Yes, I think so. I want to know, Justin. Something terrible is going on around here.'

'Very well,' he said. He looked away from me, as though wrestling with his conscience. 'I suppose you have to know. Especially after what happened to you tonight.' He studied me for a moment. 'Did you ever hear of 'Rappaccini's Daughter'?'

The name sounded vaguely familiar but I couldn't quite place it. 'Hawthorne,' Justin explained.

Of course. It was a short story by Nathaniel Hawthorne. I'd read it years and years ago. I couldn't possibly remember, though, what it had been about. I nodded my head slowly. 'Yes, I've read it, but I don't remember it. Why? What does Nathaniel Hawthorne have to do with Sarah?'

'I just thought if you remembered the story it might help you to understand about Sarah Braddock.' He paused before continuing. 'Rappaccini was a scientist who fathered a young girl, Beatrice. He also kept a strange garden — one in which he grew and cultivated plants that devoured life. Rappaccini's wife died, leaving Beatrice to her father's devilish wiles. He nursed the young child on the deadly plants in his garden. Beatrice grew up with the hideous power of killing anything she breathed upon.'

I shuddered. 'Yes, I remember now. She drank poison and died at her lover's feet rather than harm him.'

'Yes, that's right.'

'But what does all this have to do with Sarah?'

'This might all sound rather bizarre to you, but you must believe I'm telling you the truth.' He faltered as though screwing up his courage. 'Young Sarah is very much like Rappaccini's daughter. She has the same capacity as those carnivorous plants we showed you in the garden greenhouse.'

My eyes went wide. 'What are you saying? That isn't possible. 'Rappaccini's Daughter' was merely fiction. Beatrice didn't exist. She was a figment of Hawthorne's imagination.'

'But Sarah is real. And like Beatrice, she can kill.'

'You're insane,' I almost yelled.

Justin cast a worried look toward the door. 'Be quiet,' he urged. 'Don't let them hear you.'

'I don't care who hears me. You can't keep a child cooped up like that and invent some ridiculous story just to appease your guilty consciences.'

'Alice, please. Calm yourself. I'm not

inventing anything. What do you think happened to you tonight? Why did you become unconscious when you were talking to Sarah? What happened to you? Think about it a moment. Why did you become so very weak and then pass out?'

I couldn't think for a moment. Then suddenly I remembered the milk. 'The milk,' I said hurriedly. 'Diana gave me milk to make me sleep. She most likely put a heavy sleeping draught in it.'

'No, she did no such thing. It was Sarah. Sarah sapped your strength. And if I hadn't come upon you when I did she would have taken the very life right out of your body.'

I stared at him as though he were a lunatic. 'But that's absolutely ridiculous,' I managed to say.

'It isn't ridiculous. It's true, unfortunately, all too true. Sarah has the power to steal life and breath from human beings . . . from anything that lives.'

I shook my head violently. 'I don't believe you. I won't believe you.'

Justin grabbed my shoulders and shook me gently. 'You must believe me, Alice.

You must never go near that solarium again, ever. Do you hear me? Sarah almost killed you tonight and she will try again if you persist on going back to her.'

'That's insane. Sarah wouldn't harm a fly.'

'You must believe what I'm telling you. Please.'

I shook my head. How could he expect me to believe such a preposterous lie? No, it wasn't Sarah I was suddenly afraid of — it was them . . . all of them . . . Leland, Justin, even my own mother. They were keeping that child locked up here in Falcon House for some devilish purpose. What, I didn't know, but I certainly could not — would not — believe that young Sarah was capable of sucking life out of living things. It was too absurd.

'This evening I waited for you in the downstairs salon,' Justin said. 'I wanted to explain everything to you. I thought you had a right to know and I had to warn you. I waited and waited, and suddenly I thought that perhaps you'd gone back to talk again to Sarah. When I went to the solarium, Sarah had you on the bed and

137

was rapidly draining life from your body. I had no other alternative but to render her unconscious by pressing the motor vein in her neck. I carried you here just minutes before I heard Leland and Diana returning from their hunt.'

'Their what?'

Justin looked annoyed with himself. 'I shouldn't have mentioned that.' He let out a deep sigh. 'Leland and Diana hunt for wild game, animals to sustain Sarah's life.'

I stared at him. Again I cringed away, recoiling against the headboard of the bed.

Justin couldn't look at me. 'I know it's monstrous, but it's true. Sarah can't live on normal food. It is Leland's only way of keeping her alive.'

'I don't want to hear any more,' I said. 'I won't listen.'

'You must listen. You must and you will.' He shook me hard. 'Don't be such a little fool. It's for your own good. When Sarah was a mere child,' he went on, 'she stumbled into the greenhouse where Leland grows his carnivorous plants, the ones we showed you. She was only a tiny tot, no more than a few years old. Like all small children she was inquisitive. She happened to find a bottle containing a formula Leland used for feeding and nurturing the Drosera flowers. Sarah drank it. Leland found her lying in the bed of Drosera plants. The leaves had completely enveloped her. She was barely alive when Leland cut her free. She was unconscious for many weeks, in a coma. Although her experience didn't prove fatal to Sarah, it was soon clear that Sarah had the power to sap the life from every living thing that came within contact of her.

'It's a strange power. Sarah can activate it at will. She doesn't kill unless she wants to kill. Her mind is what motivates her homicidal tendencies. When she is asleep or unconscious she's completely harmless. That's why Martin hit her when she was running away. He had to knock her unconscious. He had no other recourse.'

I shook my head again. 'Stop it, Justin. I won't listen to you. You're lying to me.'

'Why would I lie to you? Don't be a

fool, Alice. I'm only telling you all of this for your own good. I'm trying to keep you from harm. Listen to me, please. You must not go near Sarah ever again. Promise me.'

I lowered my eyes. 'I can't promise you,' I said firmly. 'I intend getting Sarah out of this terrible house if it's the last thing I do.'

'No. Please don't do this, Alice. At least not for a while. Stay away from her for just a little while longer. Then . . . ' He didn't finish.

'Then, what? What are you planning for her?' I asked. My eyes narrowed with suspicion. 'You mustn't hurt that child, Justin. I'm warning you. If anything happens to Sarah I'll go to the authorities.'

'You don't know what you're saying. I'm working on a possible cure for her. If it works we'll be only too happy to put Sarah out into the world where she belongs. Until then she must stay where she is, regardless of the cost.'

His eyes were leveled on me. 'I think I've found a formula, a potion, which will bring Sarah back to normal,' he said. 'I plan on giving it to her the first chance I get. I don't want Leland and Diana to know about it because Leland is afraid an untested cure might kill Sarah. But I must try. I've locked Sarah in again and injected her with a sedative. I didn't mention your visiting Sarah to Leland or Diana and I'd appreciate you not saying anything to them just yet. They would only worry and be more upset than they are. They know it was Sarah you saw running across the field and the fear of your exposing her existence in this house has them both at the point of hysteria, especially Leland. He knows if the authorities find out about Sarah's malady they'll have her put away someplace.'

I didn't want to look at him any more. This nonsense about her capacity to kill was outlandish nonsense. Justin was afraid of her for some other reasons, reasons earthly and real and ordinary. He wasn't afraid she'd sap life from living beings, he was afraid for some other reason and I had the feeling that reason had to do with the Braddock money.

He'd invented his fantastic story in order to lure me away from Sarah.

He started to talk again but I held up my hand.

'Please, Justin. I'm tired. It's been a terrible night. I must get some sleep.'

'Of course,' he said softly, patting my hand. 'Get to sleep, Alice. We'll talk again in the morning.'

I couldn't force myself to return his smile. Tomorrow I'd go to Sarah and I would get her out of Falcon House if I had to die in the attempt.

11

The moment I opened my eyes I felt a cold dampness all around me. Somewhere across the gulf a church bell was tolling. Its ominous, slow clanging reminded me of a funeral knell.

I lay there trying to shake off the weary feeling that permeated my body. My mind wouldn't cooperate for a moment or two. I knew where I was, but the lethargy of my brain wouldn't permit me to remember anything else.

The stillness of the room was like that of a mausoleum. I ran my hands through my hair and tried to shake off the heavy leaden feeling that seemed to be holding me down. The bell, far and remote, continued to toll; its sound echoed across the water, drifting through my little room.

I rolled onto my side and felt the weight of my leg cast roll with me. Slowly I pushed back the coverlet and tried to concentrate on the day, the hour, the place. I was in Falcon House. It was morning. I tried to think. Sunday. Sunday morning.

Get up, Alice, a voice said somewhere back in the cobwebs of my mind. Get up. There is so much you must do.

Yes, I had to get up, I said to myself. Whatever had to be done, I should be up doing it. The lethargy that I found myself wrapped in was so weighty, like the plaster cast on my leg. I shook my head and tried to clear away the mist.

I swung the heavy leg cast over the side of the bed, forcing the other leg to follow suit, and sat there, head in hands. I glanced at the nightstand and saw the empty milk glass sitting there, reminding me.

The drug. The sleeping potion. Yes, Diana had given me warm milk and it had made me unconscious. No, that wasn't it. Justin had made me drink something too. I straightened. Justine had been here, in this room. Justin had said . . . Sarah.

My back went stiff. Sarah. I had to get her out of this house. It all started to come back to me now. Justin wanted to harm her. I had to get her away before something terrible happened.

I got to my feet and instantly I swayed and sat back down on the bed. Whatever I drank had indeed been potent. Had Diana really drugged me?

It couldn't possibly have been little Sarah. What a preposterous lie Justin had wanted me to believe.

Again I chanced getting to my feet. This time I moved more slowly and stood, teetering slightly, but I maintained my balance and went toward the bathroom, bracing myself against table, bureau, door jamb, sink.

I almost didn't recognize the face reflected in the mirror. I looked so drawn, so haggard. I splashed cold water against my face and blotted it with a fluffy towel.

It didn't really matter how I looked, I told myself. The important thing was to get Sarah out of Falcon House before . . . before *what?* I couldn't answer that question, yet I was sure her life was in danger.

The hallway was ominously quiet as I

limped along without benefit of crutch or cane. I found I could manage better without either support.

Diana and Leland's room stood open. I went to the doorway and peeked in. I called Diana's name, then Leland's. No answer. They were most likely at breakfast. According to my watch, it was a little past ten o'clock.

The house was as silent as a tomb, not the slightest hint of sound. Nothing moved, nothing creaked, nothing jostled. Even the elevator itself didn't jerk or groan this morning as I rode it down to the first floor. It was as if someone had put a pall on Falcon House.

The bright, gay salon was empty. It too had a slightly drab look this morning. The terrace was unoccupied, the dining room vacant, as was the kitchen area. There wasn't a solitary soul anywhere.

The church bell started to toll again. Sunday, I thought. Yes, it was Sunday. Hattie and Martin were most likely off today. Diana and Leland possibly could be attending services at the local church. Perhaps Justin was with them.

My eyes automatically moved upward toward the ceiling, toward the floor above and the glassed-in solarium. Sarah would be alone. Perhaps this was the right moment. My stomach was crying out for something to eat but I had to ignore it. I didn't have time to eat anything now. If I were to get Sarah successfully out of Falcon House I would have to move fast. The time was perfect.

I'd throw some essentials into a small bag, then go and collect young Sarah. I went up to my room and started to throw together the things I'd need to make good our escape.

Suddenly my hands froze on the latches of the suitcase as I was about to close it. What if Sarah and I ran head on into Leland's boat returning from services? What would I say? How could I explain? Perhaps it would be better if I waited for them to return so that I'd know where they were. Perhaps I'd best wait until after dinner before attempting to spirit Sarah off Falcon Island unseen.

I couldn't chance having our escape foiled. Quickly I locked my suitcase and pushed it back into the closet. It would be safe there until I needed it later on. For now I would go and tell Sarah to get herself ready to leave this evening.

I didn't feel right about sneaking away as I planned on doing, but it was the only thing I could do. I had to get Sarah away. Afterward we could sit down and talk about what to do next. We'd go directly to the sheriff's office at Gulf Point. After he heard Sarah's story he'd have no other recourse but to help us.

Again I went down the corridor toward the south wing. The house seemed to be coming back to life. Boards creaked, a soft breeze fluttered the curtains of the hall's half-opened windows. I stepped into the darkness of the south wing and went, as quickly as my cast would permit, down through the maze of hallways until I reached the door leading to the solarium. Again I was surprised to find the door in the glass wall standing ajar.

'Sarah,' I called softly. 'Sarah.'

No answer.

I went toward the open door. As the light of the room hit me full face, I stopped dead in my tracks. I stared. There, lying on the floor was Justin Braddock. He was on his back, his eyes were closed, his arms outstretched. I gasped and hurried toward him, staring down. His face was the color of death. His mouth was opened slightly but I could see no signs of breathing, no indication of life in his body.

A cold shiver suddenly raced up and down my back as my hand went to my throat. I couldn't move. I merely stood staring, trying not to listen to the horrible thoughts that were running through my mind.

Then I heard a soft, low moan. But it wasn't Justin who moaned. It came from the corner of the room. I looked around. Sarah was tangled up in her bedclothes. She groaned again and started to uncurl herself.

'Sarah,' I said quickly, rushing to help her.

I sat down on the edge of the bed and gathered her into my arms. Like Justin, she was the color of death. Her eyes were glazed over, her cheeks ashen, her mouth pale and drawn. I ran my hands through her hair and waited anxiously for her to collect herself. She just rested against me, breathing deeply.

'What happened?' I asked, shifting my gaze to Justin who lay inert on the floor just inside the door.

She pushed herself away from me. Our eyes met. She studied me for a moment — as I was studying her.

'He's dead,' Sarah said softly. 'Uncle Justin is dead.'

12

'Dead!' I breathed. I glanced at Justin's body and started to get up, but Sarah clung to me.

'Don't leave me,' she cried. 'I'm so afraid.'

I wrapped my arms about her and again smoothed down her hair and nervously caressed her. 'There, there, Sarah,' I said. I was shaking all over but I had to be strong for her. 'Try not to think of it. Don't look at him, Sarah.'

'It was horrible,' Sarah sobbed. 'Daddy made him die. Daddy killed him.'

'Leland?' I gasped.

'Oh, Alice. It was so terrible.'

I tried hard to keep myself under control. Finding Justin dead was shock enough without the knowledge that his own brother was responsible for his death. I eased Sarah gently away from me and tilted her head up. 'You'd better tell me exactly what happened here,' I said.

Sarah covered her face with her hands. 'I don't want to talk about it,' she cried.

'You must, Sarah. You'd best try to compose yourself and tell me everything. You will have to tell it all to the police anyway.'

Her head shot up. 'The police?' Her eyes were wide as saucers.

'I'll have to notify them, of course,' I said, trying to keep my voice from sounding too nervous. I had to stay calm.

'No, you mustn't do that. You mustn't tell the police.' She grabbed my arms and began shaking me. 'Please, Alice. You mustn't tell the police.'

'Listen. It's going to be all right, Sarah. I must notify the authorities. I haven't any other choice. Besides,' I added, pausing and trying to think rationally, 'it's for your own good.'

'What do you mean?'

'It will get you out of this prison you're being kept in. It will accomplish that at least.'

Sarah didn't say anything. She was merely studying me. It was difficult to interpret the expression on her face. It was a mixture of pleasure and fear. It was a strange look.

'You'd better start from the beginning, dear,' I said. 'Tell me what happened.'

Sarah looked down at her hands in her lap. She tangled her fingers together and sat there for a moment lacing and unlacing them. 'Well,' she started finally. 'I had been working on picking the lock earlier this morning. And I picked it, too,' she boasted childishly. Again she looked away from me. 'The door was open and I was coming to find you, but Uncle Justin caught me before I had a chance to leave this room.'

She glanced around the solarium with an expression of hatred. Slowly her gaze returned to her lap. 'He wanted me to drink some kind of medicine. He said it would make me well. I told him I wasn't sick, but he said that I was, and that I must drink his medicine.' Again she looked up at me with her frightened little face. 'He tried to force me. And he hurt me too,' she added, holding out her wrists to show the ugly red marks they bore. 'See.'

'Oh, no,' I gasped when I saw the bruises on her arms.

'Then, Daddy came in,' she went on. 'Daddy yelled at him and told him to leave me alone. He grabbed Uncle Justin and pulled him away from me. Uncle Justin was trying to convince Daddy that I needed the medicine and Daddy wouldn't let him give it to me. Then Daddy told Uncle Justin that if the medicine was so harmless, he should take some of it himself just so Daddy would be sure it wouldn't hurt me.' She fanned out her hands and shrugged her shoulders. 'So Uncle Justin drank it and then he died.'

She said the last sentence so casually, so unconcernedly that I could do nothing but stare at her.

'I guess I fainted or something,' she added meekly.

I sat there for a moment trying to think, trying to absorb everything she'd told me. It was as though I were living a nightmare.

'Where's your father now?' I asked, trying desperately to sound calm.

'I don't know. He ran away. I guess he went for a doctor or something.'

I stood up quickly, trying not to look at Justin's body, and pulled Sarah to her feet. 'You'd better come along with me,' I said sharply. 'It's about time we had a showdown with your father.'

Sarah suddenly wrenched herself out of my grip. 'No,' she said loudly and firmly. 'No, I can't. I won't go with you to Daddy. He'll punish me. He always punishes me whenever I leave my room. He'll beat me like always.'

'No, he won't, Sarah. I won't let him. I'll be with you. It'll be all right.'

'No,' Sarah insisted, avoiding my hand when I reached for her again. 'You go and find Daddy. You tell him and bring him back here so he can see I didn't leave my room. Then he won't punish me. You bring Daddy back here.'

It was easy enough to see that she was deathly afraid of meeting her father outside the confines of the solarium. I wondered idly what she would be like once I'd managed to spirit her off Falcon Island. But I didn't have to worry about

155

that now. The authorities would take care of Sarah — as well as Leland and Diana.

'Very well, Sarah. But you stay here. Don't run away. I'll be back in a few minutes.'

'I'll stay here, Alice,' she promised. Suddenly she grabbed my hand. 'Hurry, please. I'm so afraid.'

'I'll hurry,' I promised and rushed out of the room, leaving Sarah slumped on the bed.

As I hurried along through the maze of halls and corridors of Falcon House, I tried to think of the outcome. One consolation was the fact that Sarah would be free and happy. Justin accomplished that much, I thought, even though it had cost him his life.

The door to Diana and Leland's room was still ajar, but the room remained empty. I called their names loudly, angrily and heard an answer from downstairs. I turned and went back along the corridor to the top of the crazy-quilt staircase. Leland was in the center of the entrance hall, looking up at me.

'What's wrong, Alice. Why are you

yelling?' he asked.

'You know perfectly well what's wrong, Leland,' I shouted down at him. 'You'd better call the sheriff's office right away.' I leveled my eyes at him and jutted out my chin. 'And if you won't call the sheriff, then I will.'

'The sheriff,' he gasped. 'You'd better explain, Alice. What are you talking about?'

My temper flew out of control. He was trying to put me off again. Well he wouldn't succeed this time. I huffed away from the top of the stairs and went toward the private elevator. All the way down to the first level I was fighting to keep my temper in check.

Leland was still standing where I'd left him as I limped off the elevator.

'Now please explain what's going on, Alice.'

'You know perfectly well, Leland. And don't say I'm imagining things again.'

Leland's face was as innocent as a baby's, but he wouldn't fool me with that innocence. Justin was dead and he was responsible.

'Alice. Tell me. Why are you so upset?'

'I found Justin's body,' I hissed. 'That's why I'm so upset.' My hands were firmly planted on my hips. My chin was jutted out in defiance.

'Justin's body?' he gasped. 'What on earth are you talking about?'

'In Sarah's room — the solarium upstairs. He's dead, Leland. Dead!' I shouted the word. 'And don't play the innocent with me. You know perfectly well what I'm talking about. Sarah told me everything.'

'Sarah?'

'Yes, Sarah. She told me everything.' I stood squarely in front of him. 'Well, are you going to call the sheriff's office or am I?'

'Alice, please. Control yourself. I don't really know what you're talking about. Justin got up very early and said he was going back to the university to do some work in his lab.'

'Oh, Leland.' I spun away from him and went quickly toward the telephone. 'Give me the sheriff's office in Gulf Point,' I said quickly when the operator answered.

'Yes, Miss Whelan,' the sheriff said, 'What can I do for you?'

'I think you'd better come out here right away. There's been a death.' I turned to see Leland's expression, but the entrance hall was empty. Leland was gone.

'A death?' the sheriff asked. 'Whose death?'

'Justin Braddock's,' I told him. 'I found his body only minutes ago. You'd better hurry out.'

'This isn't some kind of practical joke, is it, Miss Whelan? Are you sure you're feeling all right?'

'Now look, Sheriff,' I said in a huff. 'I'm not the kind of person who plays practical jokes and if I were I certainly would not think up something as horrible as murder.'

'Murder? I thought you said a death?'

'I think it's murder,' I told him evenly. 'Justin Braddock is dead. I found his body in the solarium upstairs. I have every reason to believe he's been poisoned.'

'Poisoned?' I heard his hand go over

the mouthpiece. There was a pause. After a second or two he came back on the line. 'All right, Miss Whelan. We'll be right out. Now don't you run away, Miss Whelan,' he added quickly. 'We'll want to talk especially to you when we get there.'

'I'll be here,' I promised.

'You're sure you aren't merely imagining all this, Miss Whelan?' he asked.

'I am not imagining it.' I dropped the receiver back into its cradle and hurried across the entrance hall to the bright yellow and orange salon. It was empty. Leland had obviously gone to Sarah.

Again I went back up on the elevator. Just as I stepped out into the second floor corridor I saw Diana coming out of my room.

'Oh, there you are, dear,' she said. 'I was just looking for you.' She came toward me. When she noticed my wary expression her smiled faded. 'Alice? What is it?' She touched my arm.

I couldn't help myself. I pulled away from the touch of her hand.

'Justin's dead,' I said through clenched teeth.

Her hand flew up to her throat. Her eyes widened in alarm. 'Justin? Dead? Alice, what are you saying?'

'Just that. He's dead, Mother, and Leland is responsible.'

'Alice, no. You mustn't make up such cruel things. You don't know what you're talking about.' Her face was white as a sheet.

'I'm not imagining anything this time,' I said evenly. 'I found Justin's body in the solarium when I went to see Sarah.'

'Sarah?' she gasped. 'No, Alice. No.'

'Yes, Sarah,' I said defiantly. 'And don't tell me I'm imagining Sarah too. Sarah's the girl I saw at Gulf Point. I saw Martin strike her. I didn't imagine any of it, as you all wanted me to believe. I saw her and I looked for her and I found her.' Diana merely stood there, gaping.

'I've called Sheriff Anderson,' I said. 'He'll be here shortly.'

'Oh, Alice,' she moaned. 'You mustn't do this. You don't know what you're doing, child.'

'I know perfectly well what I'm doing Mother. You've kept a poor unfortunate

161

girl hidden away in this house for too long. The authorities will deal with you and Leland for all the terrible things you've done to Sarah.'

'Alice, no. You don't know what you're saying. You don't understand.'

'I understand perfectly well.'

'You foolish, foolish girl,' she said in a broken voice. 'You don't know what you've done. You just don't know.' She turned finally and walked — as in a trance — back to her room and closed the door.

I started toward her room. But I had to go to Sarah first. I'd try to make amends with Mother later on. My first duty was to Sarah. Leland mustn't harm her in any way. He mustn't punish her.

I turned and went quickly toward the south wing. I retraced my steps back to the hot, humid solarium. When I reached the door I found it standing open. I hurried into the room.

There was no Sarah, no Leland. There was no Justin.

The room was empty.

13

Empty. There was no one, no body, nothing. I stood there clutching my throat, squeezing back the scream that threatened to rush out of me. Was I losing my mind? I wondered, pushing my fingers back through my hair. Was it true that I was only imagining things?

I had called Sheriff Anderson who would be here with his deputy at any moment. No matter what I did or said, after this they'd be totally convinced that my near fatal airplane accident had managed to unhinge my mind. Nobody would believe me now. Everyone would think me deranged, if not mad.

I had to find Sarah. If I could only locate Sarah, she'd be able to substantiate everything. There was no use my turning to Diana or to Leland. They wanted everyone to believe I fantasized. They would do anything and everything they could to put suspicion on my mental stability.

I had to stay calm. I had to stay rational and think clearly. I mustn't let my nerves unravel now.

Somewhere behind me I heard the creak of a door being shut, and the sounds of hurried but muffled footsteps. The sounds brought me out of my dilemma. I turned, went back out into the dim corridor and started toward the main part of the house, and hesitated. If Leland was spiriting Sarah away he would not have gone that way for fear of meeting me. He'd go down the back stairs.

My nerves tightened as I went toward the back stairway. I began wondering what I'd find at the bottom of the staircase. As it turned out, I found nothing. The pantry was empty, the kitchen was empty.

I looked around. Perhaps there was a cellar. To me, it seemed the most likely place for someone to hide a body. A house this size and this old most assuredly was built over a cellar. I began opening and closing doors, finding larders, closets, storage rooms.

Behind one door, however, I found a wooden stairway leading down. I stood, peering down into the darkness below. There was no sound, no sign of movement. A light cord hung from a socket at the head of the stairs. I yanked it but the bulb did not light. I pulled the cord several times with no results. The darkness below seemed to become gloomier.

Determined to continue my search, I turned back into the kitchen and began rummaging through drawers until I found a candle and some matches. My hands were trembling so badly it took three matches before I managed to light the wick. Then, shielding the light with a cupped palm, I went back toward the cellar stairs.

Cautiously I made my way down the creaking stairs, step by step. My hand touched a square wooden railing. The wood felt rough and dusty; the cellar was obviously not used very often . . . if at all.

Suddenly I heard a sound, dull and unrecognizable. I held my candle high and peered around. I saw nothing, just the usual clutter of crates and barrels and thick, dusty cobwebs one usually finds in forgotten cellars.

I heard the thud again. It seemed to come from up ahead. I walked more slowly, more cautiously, keeping one eye to the front, at the same time glancing down to make sure not to trip over anything that might lie discarded in my path.

Again the thudding sound. I looked up and saw what caused the noises. A small cellar window up near the beams was banging softly in the ocean breeze. The panes were too encrusted with grime to see any daylight beyond.

A sudden draft almost blew out my candle. I protected the flame with my hand and looked to see what had caused the sudden draft. I found I had walked directly in front of a wide-mouthed arch that appeared to be the entrance of a tunnel. I stood at the mouth of the tunnel until my eyes grew adjusted to the darkness. A massive passageway yawned before me, with a barrel-shaped roof many feet high. I must have walked beyond the exterior walls of Falcon House.

I walked for several hundred feet before I came to the tunnel's end. I found myself standing at the bottom of still another stairway, this one made of slabs of rock. The top of the staircase — what I could see of it — seemed to go up into nowhere.

I started up. As I climbed I found the vaulted ceiling getting closer and closer to the top of my head. The stairs ended at an overhead trap-door. I laid my hand on the heavy panel of wood and pushed — with some difficulty — upward. A warm, damp gush of air descended down over me as I raised the door and started to crawl up.

The dampness grew more and more intense. I left the tunnel staircase and went up into the light. When I glanced around I saw that I was in the garden greenhouse — that hot, humid glass house where Leland and Justin grew their horrible plants and flowers.

I eased the trap door back into place and stood there gazing at the rows upon rows of plant growth, trying to get my bearings, thinking back on my last visit to the place. I decided that the Droseras were directly behind me. I didn't want to look at them, yet something nagged at me to search them out. Slowly I turned my head.

A scream broke from my throat when I felt a rough hand grab me. My entire body went stiff as the blood drained down to my feet. Someone spun me around. Martin pulled me close to him. His face was creased in an angry scowl. His hands dug into the softness of my arms.

'What are you doing here?' he demanded in a growl.

I couldn't speak. I just stared up at him with eyes riveted in fear.

He shook me hard. 'What are you doing here, I said?'

The whole place was suddenly swimming around me. I thought I was going to faint. I wouldn't, I told myself firmly. I mustn't faint. I mustn't. I fell against him.

'Martin,' I managed to gasp. My voice sounded so far, far away.

He continued to scowl down at me. 'Get out of here. Get back to the house.'

I hung there in his arms. I couldn't move. I could feel his rough, hard fingers digging painfully into my flesh. It hurt, but I knew if he released me I'd fall to the floor. I tried to speak again but my throat was still too tight with fear.

'You frightened me almost to death,' I said in short, jagged breaths.

'Get away from here,' he growled. 'You have no business in here.'

I started to feel strength seep back into my muscles. I straightened up and pushed away from him. 'I was looking for Mr. Braddock,' I told him breathlessly.

'He is not here. Go back where you belong.'

The thought didn't occur to me until after a few minutes that if I were in danger from Leland, it was just as possible that Martin represented the same danger. They were obviously in this thing together — whatever this *thing* was. I couldn't let him intimidate me. I refused to have him order me away.

'I must find Leland Braddock and his daughter.'

Martin's eyes widened. His lower jaw

fell slightly. 'His daughter?' he gasped.

'Yes,' I said, leveling my eyes at him. 'And you know where Sarah is,' I told him defiantly.

'I don't know what you are talking about.'

But he did know; I could tell by the look on his face that he knew perfectly well what I was talking about.

'You know precisely what I'm talking about, Martin. Mr. Justin has been killed and the sheriff is on his way here at any moment. If you chose to involve yourself any deeper in this affair with the Braddock family you have my promise that I'll involve you.'

'You're as loony as they say you are,' he said.

He grabbed my arm. 'Go back to the house, Miss Alice,' he said. This time I noticed that the growl was gone out of his voice. He almost sounded as though he were pleading with me.

'Not until I find Sarah.'

The sound of a boat motor seemed to vibrate the glass panels of the hothouse. It would be the sheriff's boat, I told myself.

I had to find Sarah if I wanted to save myself in the eyes of the authorities.

Martin dragged me toward the front entrance of the building.

'Let me go,' I cried, struggling to wrench myself free of Martin's grip. My struggles were in vain. I'd seen Sarah fighting against this man, and like Sarah, I was no match for his powerful strength. He pulled me easily along after him.

Martin half dragged me back toward the house. He didn't release me until he had me through the dining room and out into the entrance hall where Diana and Leland were standing waiting for Sheriff Anderson.

'There you are, Alice,' Diana said, oblivious to the fact that Martin was manhandling me and had shoved me toward them with such force that I almost toppled at their feet. Her look was as cold as frost on glass. 'The Sheriff's launch is here,' she continued icily. 'I do wish you would have consulted us before calling him. It is so very embarrassing for all of us. Especially you, my dear.'

'Where's Sarah?' I demanded.

Diana touched his arm and leveled her eyes to mine. 'You're hysterical, child,' she said. 'You're imagining things again. There is no one here named Sarah.'

'That's a lie and you know it. I've talked to her. I've seen her.'

Leland let out a deep sigh and slowly turned to look at me. 'You have seen no one,' he said firmly. 'I'm afraid the airplane accident has left you more dazed than we imagined. I suppose you really should be sent back to the hospital where they can look after you.'

'You can't frighten me, Mr. Braddock. I know your ugly secret and I intend to shout it to the world if I have to.'

'Alice,' Diana said softly. 'Please try to control yourself. You're only making matters worse for yourself.'

'I don't care about myself. If it's the last thing I do, I'll . . . '

Diana raised an imperious hand. 'That will do, Alice,' she said angrily. 'We have had just about enough of your tantrums. Be still. Sheriff Anderson is coming across the terrace. Try not to make yourself look any more foolish than you are right now.'

Her rebuke managed to stem my so-called tantrum, but it did not stem my determination. I had enough Diana Hamilton in me to make myself a worthy opponent for her. I couldn't let my father's side of me show through. Diana was too expert in dealing successfully with the gentler side of my personality — just as she had dealt with my father.

Leland opened the front door before Sheriff Anderson had a chance to knock. The sheriff stood there with one of his deputies. They both looked frighteningly grim.

'Ah, Sheriff Anderson,' Leland said pleasantly. 'How nice to see you,' he added, putting out his hand. Leland shook hands with both men. 'You both know my wife, of course,' he said, smiling at Diana.

The men bowed to the royal presence. 'And my stepdaughter,' Leland added, indicating me with a nod.

'We've spoken on the telephone,' the sheriff clarified. 'How are you Miss Whelan?'

'Sheriff . . . '

Diana interrupted. 'I'm afraid this might prove a bit awkward, Sheriff Anderson. My daughter, I'm sorry to say, has brought you out here through some misunderstanding.'

'Poison isn't exactly my idea of a misunderstanding, Miss Hamilton . . . Mrs. Braddock.' The sheriff turned a skeptical eye to me. 'Or were you imagining things again, Miss Whelan?'

'No, I was not . . . '

Again Diana cut me off. 'Not exactly,' she said politely. 'I'm afraid my daughter has been under a terrible strain these past several weeks . . . the airplane accident and all. Actually, Alice here has never really been a well child.'

I glowered at her but said nothing. I'd bide my time and then strike when it would hurt the most.

'Leland's brother, Justin,' Diana continued. 'Well, he had a fall this morning and struck his head. Alice found him unconscious and thought he'd done himself a serious injury. Fortunately it proved to be nothing, nothing at all.'

'That's not true and you know it,' I said

174

in anger. I turned quickly back to Sheriff Anderson. 'If what she's saying is true, ask her where Justin is now.'

Leland spoke up. 'Why, he went back to the university.' He turned and saw my narrowed eyes, my set jaw. 'If you don't believe me, Alice dear, call the university and ask.'

The sheriff and his deputy shifted their weight from foot to foot.

'All right, I will,' I said, calling his bluff.

Martin was standing in the background. When I turned toward the telephone he walked ahead of me and reached it first. He picked up the receiver and held it out to me. I wanted to slap the smug expression off his face.

'I'm afraid the university switchboard is closed, Miss. Today is Sunday, you know,' the operator told me after I'd asked to be connected.

Of course, I thought, with a sinking feeling in the pit of my stomach. It was Sunday. They'd let me make a still bigger fool of myself.

14

It took a few seconds for me to find the courage to turn and face them. They were all looking at me. I thought I recognized a look of pity on Diana's face. I didn't need her pity, I told myself. I didn't want it.

'The university switchboard is closed on Sunday,' I said, and I knew I looked and sounded beaten. I gritted my teeth. I wouldn't let them defeat me. I had to stand up to them, all of them.

Leland made a helpless gesture. He turned to Sheriff Anderson and smiled weakly. 'Perhaps you could stop at the university when you go back. My brother said he would be working in the laboratory today.'

'I'll do that,' the sheriff answered. I could tell he was more than just a little annoyed.

I tried to think of something to say, something to do to prevent the sheriff from leaving. If he found Sarah she could verify Justin's death.

'I'm so very sorry you and your deputy have been put to this inconvenience,' Diana put in. She glanced at me, then back to the sheriff. 'Try to understand, Sheriff. Alice has been through such a terrible ordeal.'

'I understand,' he said politely. 'Well, come on, Joe. We've wasted enough time as it is.'

'Wait,' I called out. They all turned and looked at me again.

'Well?' the Sheriff said gruffly.

'There's a girl kept prisoner in this house,' I blurted out.

Diana stiffened. Leland gave an exasperated sigh. 'Really, Alice,' he said.

I ignored him. I rushed up to Sheriff Anderson. I didn't care what any of them thought of me at this point. Justin's body had to be found. Sarah had to be rescued. 'I'm telling you the truth,' I said hurriedly. 'Her name is Sarah. She was a witness to Justin Braddock's death. They've hidden her away some place. I've been searching for her but I can't find her.'

'Now look, Miss Whelan,' the sheriff started.

'Please,' I urged, tugging at his arm. 'At least look around. I promise I won't cause you any more inconvenience if you'll just search the house. I know she's here. I've seen her. I've talked to her. They're lying to you,' I added, including Diana, Leland, and Martin with a sweep of my hand.

'Alice, please,' Diana pleaded. 'You're only making yourself look more ridiculous.'

The sheriff and Leland exchanged looks. I saw Leland shrug. His shoulders sagged. 'Perhaps, just to humor the child,' he said to the sheriff and his deputy, 'you might look around.'

Sheriff Anderson hesitated. He studied me for a moment then glanced at Diana.

She nodded and tried to smile with her eyes. 'Please,' she said softly.

The sheriff suddenly looked flushed. 'Well, if you think it will help.' He motioned to his deputy. 'Come on, Joe. Let's have a look around.'

I knew they were going to try making a fool of me again; that couldn't be helped.

At least I had the sheriff in Falcon House. I felt determined to prove myself right.

'This way, sheriff,' I said quickly. 'They keep Sarah locked up in the solarium in the south wing. That's where I found Justin's body.'

I wasn't surprised that no one made a move to stop us. Diana stood patiently aside and let us start toward the elevator.

'Alice, dear, you really should try to stay off your leg as much as possible,' Diana said as I limped by.

'I'm all right,' I snapped. I was behaving badly, but I didn't care at the moment. All my senses were concentrated on finding Justin and Sarah. I realized that they wouldn't be in the solarium, but perhaps the sheriff and Joe might find a passageway I'd overlooked, or a room I hadn't stumbled upon.

We stood in the elevator, awkward and silent as it lifted the three of us up to the second floor. Neither Leland, Diana nor Martin made any move to come with us.

Sheriff Anderson cleared his throat as we got out of the elevator and started toward the south wing. 'Perhaps you

179

might tell us just what you think you saw, Miss Whelan,' he said.

'I didn't *think* I saw anything,' I said sharply. 'I know what I saw.'

'All right, have it your own way. Then tell us just what you say you saw.'

We went across the gallery. Glancing down I saw that Leland and Diana had gone; Martin still stood near the front door, watching us.

'If you remember,' I started, 'I called you about seeing a girl being abducted when my train arrived at Gulf Point Station the other day.'

'Yes, I remember.' He and Joe, the deputy, exchanged knowing glances. I thought I saw a trace of a smirk at the deputy's mouth.

'I remembered the car the girl was put into,' I said, 'and it was the same car that is parked at the boathouse on the other side of the gulf, Leland Braddock's limousine.' They made no comment. 'Well,' I continued in a rush, 'seeing the car, I started to put things together in my mind and I decided that the girl must have been caught by Martin and brought here to Falcon House. She was trying to escape.'

'Escape from whom?'

'Her father, Leland Braddock.'

'But Mr. Braddock doesn't have a daughter.'

'That's what he wants everyone to think.'

'I see,' he said with a resigned sigh.

I pushed through the door leading to the glass brick wall which protected the solarium.

'Here's where I found Justin's body,' I said, pointing down at the bare floor just inside the door. 'And look,' I added, motioning to the room with its toppled furniture, the furniture I myself had thrown about during my bout with frustration. 'The room is clean as a pin in comparison to those other rooms we passed.'

The sheriff merely shrugged. 'That don't mean anything,' he said. 'Maybe Mr. Braddock uses this room for some reason or other. I don't see no signs of any girl living here.'

I yanked open the door to a wardrobe.

It was empty. I hurried into the tiny, compact bathroom. The medicine cabinet was empty, the soap dish was clean and dry. There wasn't a sign at all of anyone's having occupied the room.

The sheriff and Joe looked dutifully around the little room. Then Sheriff Anderson hitched up his belt and put his hands on his broad hips. 'You said something about Justin Braddock being poisoned,' he said. 'How did you know that?'

'Sarah told me.'

He gave a disgusted little grunt. 'Oh, yeah. Sarah. I see.' Again he and Joe exchanged knowing glances.

'I was going to help Sarah escape tonight. We were planning on coming to you for help. But when I came for her this morning I found Justin's body on the floor and Sarah was just coming out of a dead faint.'

'She was just coming out of a dead faint,' the sheriff repeated. 'And she told you she saw Justin Braddock poison himself.'

'Leland Braddock made his brother

drink some kind of medicine which Justin was trying to make Sarah drink.'

'Oh, boy,' the sheriff breathed, running his hands back through his hair. 'Do you really expect me to believe that a guy would drink poison just because his brother asked him to drink poison? Now really, Miss Whelan. Why don't you go back downstairs and have your lunch and then lie down.'

'Look. I know it all sounds a bit crazy . . .'

'Crazy is right,' Joe put in.

I shot him an angry look. 'If you'll only find Sarah, she'll confirm everything I've told you.'

'You say Justin Braddock was trying to give the poison to this Sarah person? Why?'

My expression went blank. 'I don't know. He had his reasons, I suppose. He told me she wasn't well — that there was something terribly wrong with her, but I didn't believe him. He wanted to do away with Sarah for some reason or other.'

'Uh huh,' the sheriff grunted. 'Justin Braddock was trying to kill this girl

Sarah, but Sarah fainted and Justin drank the poison. I see.' He shook his head and looked down at his shoes.

'Leland made him drink it. Don't you see?'

'Frankly, Miss Whelan, I don't see. I don't see at all. And personally I think you're having some kind of hallucinations.'

'You've got to believe me,' I cried. 'Sarah is around here someplace.' It suddenly dawned on me that I might have been closer to finding Sarah when I was in the greenhouse. Martin had been standing guard in there. 'The greenhouse,' I said hurriedly. 'They've hidden her in the greenhouse.' I started out of the solarium.

'Here we go again,' the sheriff breathed, shaking his head and running his hand back through his hair. 'Now it's the greenhouse. First you take us up here to this place, now we're supposed to follow you to some greenhouse — wherever that is.'

I hurried down the corridor toward the back stairs — the route I'd followed earlier that day. I glanced back over my shoulder. My luck was holding. Despite their misgivings about my sanity, Sheriff Anderson and Joe were following me.

I felt my heart start to beat faster. I was sure I'd find Sarah locked in that other room in the greenhouse. That was why Martin had wanted me out of there. I moved down the corridor more quickly, trying to ignore the heaviness of my leg cast. From time to time I glanced back to make sure the sheriff and his deputy were behind me. They moved more slowly, Joe flashing his light into open doors, along cracked walls, over sagging ceilings.

I moved fast, not concentrating on the darkness around me. I wasn't paying any attention to where I was going. I got to the top of the back staircase. Sheriff Anderson and Joe were still behind me, moving slower, searching the rooms as they passed them. The beam of Joe's flashlight was not shining in my direction.

I didn't see the overturned chair, or whatever it was, that connected with my foot. I didn't see anything except swirling, spinning blackness as a scream tore from my throat and I toppled down. My hands flailed the air, trying to keep myself from falling. There was nothing to grab on to. There was no one close enough to save me.

I fell. My body banged hard against the stairs and blackness swept over me.

15

Dim shapes and shadows moved across the back of my eyelids. I could hear far-off voices.

'She's beginning to come around,' a strange voice said.

The room was as strange and unfamiliar as the face looming over me. Everything was white and cold and stark. I was lying on a bed with heavily starched sheets. Surrounding me were pale, staring faces. At first I recognized none of them. Then I faintly recognized the scent of her cologne.

'Darling,' she whispered, placing a cool hand on my brow. 'How are you feeling?'

'Don't move,' Diana said when I tried to turn my head. 'You've had a nasty bump, but thank goodness that's all you suffered when you fell. Sheriff Anderson caught you before you toppled down too many steps.'

'She should rest,' a voice said.

'Where am I?' The pain that shot through my head was excruciating. I blinked shut my eyes and stiffened myself against the stabbing, jarring pain.

'There, there,' Diana cooed. 'Don't talk, darling. You're in Gulf Point Hospital. You've had a nasty fall.'

The pain was returning to the back of my head. It settled there, throbbing dully.

'I'll give her a sedative,' the unfamiliar voice said. 'She'll be fine, Mrs. Braddock. Don't you worry. You should be able to take her home tomorrow.'

I felt a sharp prick in my arm.

The muffled, mumbling voices moved slightly away from me. I knew they were standing in a huddle beside my bed but I couldn't see them very clearly.

'Don't you think you should keep her here?' Diana's voice whispered.

'I see no reason for that, Mrs. Braddock.'

'Just to be sure there isn't anything internally wrong.'

'No, we've checked her thoroughly. There isn't anything seriously wrong with your daughter. I assure you, it's only a nasty bump on the head. She will be fine in no time at all.'

'But . . . '

'Come along, darling,' Leland said.

'I think I should stay with her,' Diana answered.

'She's asleep already,' the strange voice said. 'She'll sleep soundly for the rest of the night.'

'She may wake up and become frightened. As I told you, she isn't used to being around people. She's very sensitive, poor child. Her mind, you know . . . '

'From what you've both told me,' the strange voice said, 'I'd suggest your getting her under psychiatric care as soon as possible.'

'We intend to, Doctor,' Leland said. 'It will take a few days to arrange. That's why my wife and I feel Alice best remain here at the hospital until those arrangements are made.'

'I see.'

I'm here, I'm listening, I wanted to shout, but my lids were too heavy to lift and my head was too painful to move. I couldn't find my voice. The sedative was beginning to take its toll.

Psychiatrist. Arrangements. Hospital. The muffled voices began to fade. Shuffling sounds pounded in my ears. People were moving around me but I couldn't open my eyes to see who they were.

Psychiatrist. Arrangements. Hospital.

'She'll sleep until morning.'

'Come along, dear. We'll come back first thing tomorrow.'

The blackness again lifted me up and carried me away.

16

I was afraid to open my eyes. I tested to see if the pain was still lurking at the back of my head. I shifted my eyes back and forth behind my lids. The pain wasn't there — at least it didn't show itself if it were. Slowly, carefully I eased open my eyes. I lay there trying to put everything back into perspective. I found I could think. I remembered.

Psychiatrist. Arrangements. Hospital.

'No,' I said aloud. I felt braver, stronger. I darted my eyes around. I was still in the hospital room. They hadn't moved me. How long had I slept? Was it still the same day, or had I been unconscious for weeks?

Cautiously I lifted my head from the pillow and looking around, I sat up, waiting for the pain to jab at me at any second. It did not.

Moonlight was streaming in through the window. In its path lay a white metal chair, a white metal stand, a white chest of drawers with a spray of pale flowers poised on top of it. I inched my plaster cast over the side of the bed and let my other leg follow suit. I sat there, waiting. The pain threatened but it didn't break out in full fury.

I eased myself down, feeling the cold, shiny floor touch my toes and stood, bracing myself against the bed, and made my way slowly toward the window. The little town of Gulf Point slept peacefully around me. The night was muted with the purple shades of early morning. The soft, sweet smell of oleander and hibiscus wafted along undisturbed on the night air. The salty dampness of the gulf tickled my nostrils. For a moment or so I couldn't move.

Psychiatrist. Arrangements. Hospital.

The words came back to me with such force that I felt my body stiffen with fear. They'd believed I was under the narcotic influence of the sedative, but I'd heard them. I'd heard them all too clearly, planning, plotting against me. They were planning on keeping Sarah a secret from the world even if it meant confining me to a mental institution.

Diana and Leland had obviously convinced everyone that I was suffering from mental fatigue and having hallucinations. They had told everyone that my mind was coming unhinged, that I was threatened by mental unbalance. They were going to have me confined, put away, locked away — as Sarah was locked away.

I had to stop them. Sarah. I said her name aloud. 'Sarah.' She was my only hope, the only way I could prove to everyone that I wasn't crazy and imagining things. Yes, Sarah was the only answer — my only salvation.

I had to get back to Falcon Island somehow, some way — and I had to get there at once. Time was of the essence. They'd be back here tomorrow. They would give me more sedation, they would make the necessary arrangements and I would be locked up somewhere.

Quickly I went across the room and opened the closet door. My clothes were inside. I found everything I needed and then saw the small, carefully packed overnight case with my cosmetics, hair brushes and the rest of my toilet articles. It was the very same case I'd packed for my escape with Sarah. Diana had found it.

After dressing, I stood and pondered my best route of escape. The corridors would most likely be the quickest and easiest to manage, but they also might prove the most dangerous.

I went to the window and looked down. I was on the second level, but even that height made the ground seem miles and miles away. The plaster cast throbbed its objection when I stood there looking for some way to climb down. There was a convenient trellis, but it didn't look strong enough to support anything heavier than the Carolina yellow jasmine that clung to it.

At the corner of the building I saw my avenue of escape. A fire escape, painted dull red, seemed to glow softly and invitingly under the bright half moon. Judging its location, the entrance to the fire escape would be just down the hall.

I made my way back across the room and eased the door open just a crack. The overhead lights spaced along the ceiling almost blinded me and brought back the pain.

The corridor was empty. I stepped out into the bright white hallway, staying close to the wall and keeping an anxious eye out for any movement, any sound. Carefully I moved toward the end of the corridor.

Luck was with me. No one happened upon me. At the corner I hesitated and peered around. The first thing I saw was the little red light and the sign saying FIRE EXIT — but I saw something else. A man all in white coming toward me.

His head was down, studying the chart of paper he held on a clipboard. I backed up against the wall. Quickly I looked around for some place in which to disappear. Across from me was a door with a number on it. A patient's room, no doubt . . . possibly the patient for whom the doctor was headed.

I had to chance it. There was a good possibility that the room might be empty, or if not empty at least occupied by a sleeping patient. I moved quickly across the hall and darted into the room.

Again my luck held. The room was dark. There was a slumbering form in the bed. I tried not to breathe. I heard the doctor's footsteps, dull and cushioned, as he came near. Then he walked past, down along the corridor. I let out my breath.

I stayed long enough to make certain the doctor was out of sight, and no one else stepped into the corridor. After a while I peeked out. Again the corridor was empty. Quickly I slid into the hall and made my way toward the fire exit.

The night air was cool and crisp. I tried not to think about the cold; I tried not to give in to the pain that started to throb again at the back of my head. I had to move and keep on moving until I got to Falcon House and Sarah. I didn't rightly know how I expected to cross the gulf once I reached the boathouse, but I'd manage somehow.

Psychiatrist. Arrangements. Hospital. The words echoed in my mind.

Yes, I had to.

I'd only gone a short way before my leg started bothering me. My limp became more pronounced as I hobbled along. The headlights of a car suddenly came up behind me and the discomfort of my plaster cast was instantly forgotten. I practically threw myself behind some tall hedge and cowered there until the car was past.

Did I dare flag down a passing motorist? I watched the red tail lights of the first car disappear down the road. It was too far to the boathouse. I'd never make it on foot. I'd have to risk flagging a car.

As if by magic, my thought became a reality. Another car was coming slowly up behind me. Rather than hide myself again, I stepped boldly out onto the road and waved it down. It pulled up directly next to me.

'Mercy,' the old woman behind the wheel said. 'What on earth are you doing walking about at this time of night, child?'

She was an elderly woman, well past sixty, with a wrinkled yet very pleasant face and deep set eyes. Her head was wrapped in a scarf and she had a heavy cardigan draped about her shoulders.

'I was called to the hospital and couldn't get a ride back home,' I told her. 'I telephoned for a taxi cab but it never showed up.'

'That's the way they are,' she said with a huff. 'Well, get in, child. I know how it is waiting for those taxi drivers. They're sure an independent lot.'

I slipped quickly into the rider's seat, thankful to get my weight off my leg.

'Where're you headed, dearie?'

'I'm going out to Falcon Island. Do you know where that is?'

'Oh, sure. Everybody around here knows the Braddock place. I'm afraid I'm not going quite that far but I can take you almost to the boathouse.'

We rode a quarter of a mile in silence. I saw her glance at me every once in a while out of the corner of her eye.

'Somebody sick back at the hospital?' she asked.

'Yes. Nothing serious though.'

'Braddock or that new movie star wife of his?'

'No, just a friend. We're visiting at the island.'

'Visiting that place. Ugh.'

Again we drove in silence for quite a distance.

'Yeah, those taxi drivers sure don't care whether they inconvenience people or not,' she said after a while. 'Me, now. I scrub floors for a living. I can't really afford to have bought this here car, but when you work funny hours like me, you like to be sure you have a way of getting home at night. I never did trust those taxi guys anyhow. Some of them get kinda fresh, you know.'

'I know,' I said flatly, hoping not to encourage any further conversation. I didn't want to make conversation. My mind was completely taken up with the pressing matters at hand.

She must have taken the hint. She fell silent again and concentrated on her driving. She was a slow driver, but a very careful one.

I relaxed back against the seat and found myself thinking of Diana. A part of me actually felt pity for her, but she'd wanted me locked away from her when I was a child, and now again she wanted to lock me out of her life.

'Well, this is as far as I can take you, honey,' the woman said, pulling the car up to the side of the road. 'Over across that field is the shortest path through the woods. You'll see the boathouse after you go through a ways.'

* * *

The boathouse doors were locked. There were no windows through which to climb, but at the rear of the building was a small jetty with a dilapidated rowboat. It looked far from seaworthy, but I had no other means of crossing to Falcon Island. The rowboat would have to do.

I untied the little boat and settled myself down into its shell. The oars were long and heavy. Somehow I managed to fit them into the oar-locks. My head was throbbing painfully but I tried not to pay attention to it.

I pushed the boat away from the wooden pier and nosed it toward Falcon

Island. The night air was cold out on the water. A wind came up from nowhere, making my progress slower and more difficult. I pulled on the oars with all my might.

I'd never maneuvered a rowboat before and I found it was very difficult synchronizing my movements. My arms were beginning to lose their strength. I strained every muscle of my body, moving at a snail's pace. Falcon Island seemed miles and miles away.

You have to make it, I told myself. Sarah would be there waiting. We could use one of the speedboats for the trip back. We'd remove the ignition keys from whatever other boats were moored at the island pier, making it impossible for anyone to pursue us. Even if they somehow followed us to Gulf Point we would be there long before them and Sarah would tell the authorities everything. I'd be safe from the threat of an asylum. Sarah would be free to live a normal life in a normal world. Leland and Diana would get what they so richly deserved.

Push. Pull. Push. Pull.

The oars were getting heavier. The frail little craft seemed to be sinking deeper and deeper into the water. I had to hurry. I had to row faster, faster, faster.

I leaned on the oars, trying to catch my breath.

A cold wind rocked the boat. I began to row again. Falcon House crept closer and closer. The wind suddenly shifted direction and began blowing at my back, making my progress a bit easier. The boat moved faster through the water. My hands were numb on the oar handles. My legs ached unmercifully. My feet felt frozen in the cold puddle of water that kept getting deeper and deeper as I moved toward Falcon Island.

Push. Pull. Push. Pull.

The island was getting nearer. I was almost there. Another hundred yards or so and I would be at the landing.

Push. Pull. Push. Pull.

The wind got stronger. A freak storm was threatening. I glanced up at the sky and saw a dark cloud pass across the face of the half moon. I pulled harder on the oars and slid the boat across the top of the water. I had to hurry. I had to get to Falcon Island as fast as I could.

Blisters had begun to form on the palms of my hands. The muscles in my arms were screaming out for rest but I couldn't permit them to rest. I was almost there. Another few yards . . . another several feet.

The prow of the boat banged softly against the wooden piling. I'd made it. I was here. I was at Falcon Island. The rest would be easy.

I sagged as the boat thumped against the pier. I sat there for a moment, motionless, feeling the pounding in my breast. My arms were numb as I lifted the oars out of the water, slipped them from the oar-locks and laid them in the soggy bottom of the boat. The boat rocked as I lumbered out onto the pier. I dragged myself toward the house, up past the neglected swimming pool, the unkempt gardens, the terrace. The wind was bending the tree tops, sending dead leaves scurrying. I moved slowly, each step an effort.

I crossed the terrace and tried one of the French doors that led into the drawing room. The door was unlocked. I stepped inside.

The silence was intense. I stood stark still and listened. I could feel the stiffness, the soreness in every muscle of my body. The bruises on my arms and legs began to throb again; the ache at the back of my head grew worse. Yet I felt an urgency flowing through me. I had to hurry. I didn't have time to be overly cautious.

From the heavy silence surrounding me, I thought that the house was completely deserted. I moved across the drawing room to the entrance hall. A tidy dim light burned near the front door. I stared at it for a moment, wondering if Leland and Diana were again out in the woods. Surely not at this hour, I told myself, glancing up at an old Grandfather clock just inside the door. It was almost five. I had to be quick.

I considered and decided the solarium was my best bet. If Sarah wasn't there, then I could go to the greenhouse. If she wasn't in either place, then . . .

Remembering the clanging noise of the elevator, I decided on the back stairway. I realized that Martin or Hattie might well be stirring about. It was early, but perhaps they rose early.

I'd have to chance it. I stole across the entrance hall, slipped in through the dining room doors and went toward the kitchen. The rooms were all deserted and still as the grave. I reached the door to the back stairs without incident. I breathed a sigh of relief as I started up, this time being extra careful not to trip over anything, not to stumble across anything.

A stray thought suddenly drifted across my mind as I worked my way upward. What had I toppled over when I crashed down the stairs earlier? I'd used the back stairs before and had never encountered anything in my path. Had someone purposely tripped me?

There was nothing at the top of the stairs when I stepped into the corridor. Whatever had tripped me up had since been removed. But perhaps it hadn't been a 'something'; it might well have been a 'someone.' I wrapped my arms about me and limped down the dark, gloomy hallway toward Sarah's room.

I saw the chink of light shining under the door and breathed a sigh of relief. She was back in the solarium. A search for her wouldn't be necessary. She was here waiting. We could be away and in Gulf Point before the sun got too high in the sky.

I went to the door and opened it. It moved easily on its silken hinges. The wall of glittering glass greeted me. The panel door in its facade was closed. I hurried over to it and jiggled the knob lightly.

'Sarah,' I breathed. 'Sarah, it's me, Alice.'

No one answered.

I jiggled the knob again, this time more forcefully. It turned to the left. Surprisingly, it turned completely. The door was unlocked. I didn't take time to wonder why the door was unlocked. I pushed it open and went into the solarium.

Sarah was lying on the bed, her hair disheveled, her clothing loose and rumpled looking. She was breathing deeply. Her eyes were closed, her lips half parted.

'Sarah,' I said harshly, going to her and shaking her shoulder.

She didn't move.

'Sarah.' I raised my voice higher, louder.

Still she didn't move.

I stepped closer. The toe of my shoe connected with something heavy but soft just under the bed. I backed away slightly and looked down. My hands flew to my mouth. I gasped. My eyes widened in horror when I saw the inert body of a furry animal of some description stretched out on its side. Its back was to me but its head had been turned up. Its eyes were wide and glassy and its tongue lolled in its mouth.

The creature was dead. There was not the slightest doubt in my mind about that. I knelt and put a hand to its body. It was still warm. The moment I touched it I recoiled.

'Sarah,' I whispered intently, 'Sarah, get up.'

Her lids fluttered open. Her eyes looked overly shiny and glinted obscenely in the light of the room. She grinned, a long, lazy grin and stretched her arms over her head, but she did not speak.

'Sarah. Please get up. Hurry. We've got to get away,' I told her.

She curled up on one side and gave a contented sigh. 'Go away,' she mumbled. She licked her lips and sighed again. She cradled her cheek on her hands and closed her eyes.

'Sarah,' I called, shaking her violently. 'Sarah. Don't go back to sleep. Wake up. We must get away from here right now.'

She gave an annoyed shrug and licked her lips again. She tightened herself into a snug little ball and her breathing became even again.

I shook her.

'Sarah. Sarah.'

She refused to move. I couldn't awaken her.

I glanced down at the dead animal just underneath the cot and the contented expression on Sarah's face. I stared at them both in horror. Suddenly words Justin had spoken returned to my mind . . . words that had to do with Leland's hunting for wild game in order to sustain Sarah's life.

No. No. That was a preposterous story that Justin had invented. I couldn't believe that. I wouldn't believe that insane story about the Drosera plants.

And yet . . .

I took a step backward. I had to think more clearly. I'd have to let Sarah sleep for now. I had to think.

17

I started out of the room. At the doorway I paused. Again my eyes fell on the lifeless body of the animal underneath the bed. I stared at it in horror. What did it all mean? Was Justin telling me the truth when he compared Sarah to Rappaccini's daughter? But that was absurd, I told myself. Still, I couldn't help but wonder what the dead carcass of an animal was doing lying under Sarah's bed.

My spine began to tingle. Sarah looked so content, so satisfied. Perhaps everything Justin had told me was the truth. Diana and Leland had been off on their nightly hunt and had brought back the only thing that would sustain Sarah's life.

Slowly I turned my head and started down the corridor. It was useless to try and rouse Sarah. I'd have to wait. But for how long? And where?

By now the hospital would have discovered me gone. They'd be in touch with Leland and Diana first thing. The rowboat at the jetty would tell them that I'd come back to the island. They'd find me and have me committed.

The wind was stronger when I let myself out through the back entrance and skirted the terrace, going as quietly as I could toward the jetty. White peaks danced and bobbed along the surface of the gulf, whipped by the sudden wind.

My hair flew behind me as I made my way down the broken brick stairway. My leg cast was heavier than ever and made my going slow and tedious.

Once on the jetty I decided it would be impossible for me to scuttle the rowboat there. I'd have to move it and hide it. I tried not to think about the blisters on my hands or the scratches and bruises that covered my limbs. I got into the rowboat — with some difficulty — and managed to push it away from the jetty.

The wind was swirling around me. Somehow I managed to row around the bend of the beach. I began searching for some secluded place in which to conceal the boat. A clump of low hanging trees brushed the surface of the water farther up the shore. The boat slid neatly among the thick foliage, hiding itself completely. I felt the bow thump against the ground. I secured the oars and tied the boat to one of the tree branches, then scrambled out and started to make my way back toward Falcon House.

I was ravenous. I suddenly realized that I had not had anything to eat all day. It was still early. Could I possibly risk rummaging around in the kitchen for food? I moved slowly through the gum and bay trees until I came to the clearing where the greenhouse stood. I remembered the trap door leading down into the cellar. It would make a perfect hiding place until I had a chance to fetch Sarah and escape to Gulf Point.

Something or someone moved near the back entrance to Falcon House. Quickly I scurried behind a tree and peeked through the brush. Martin was walking along the path that led to the greenhouse. He was carrying something heavy. My heart sank. He didn't go into the greenhouse. Instead he skirted the corner of the building and dropped his load down onto the ground. The moment I saw him drop his parcel I recognized immediately what that parcel was. It was the carcass of the dead animal I'd seen in Sarah's room.

I watched while Martin picked up a convenient spade and started to dig into the soft, wet ground. It clearly wasn't the first time he'd dug such a grave. It was eerie standing there in the early morning light and watching a man, dressed in black, digging into the earth as a dreary mist from the gulf swirled about him. A horrifying thought suddenly crossed my mind. Had Martin dug a similar grave — larger, deeper — a grave big enough to hold the body of Justin Braddock?

I shook my head, feeling suddenly nauseous. I watched Martin replace the shovel against the side of the greenhouse and turn back toward Falcon House. The moment he was out of sight I left my hiding place among the shrubs and trees and hurried into the hot, humid interior of the greenhouse.

Hunger gnawed at me; I saw nothing

with which to satisfy it. At least I was warm and out of the clutches of the chilling wind that was blowing ever stronger. It rattled against the little house of glass, threatening to smash the panes and sweep away my refuge.

Idly I wandered over toward the bed of Drosera flowers. I stared down at them thinking of the young, frail looking girl who slept so soundly, so contentedly in that old, musty solarium.

Could all Justin said be true? Was Sarah the personification of these carnivorous Drosera flowers? I shook my head. It was no use my puzzling over something to which I could never find an answer. All that need concern me now was getting Sarah away from Falcon Island. Everything else would come to light in the natural course of events.

My stomach rumbled loudly. I had to find something to eat. I was growing too weak and I needed as much strength as possible. It might be hours before Sarah roused herself from her deep sleep and in the meantime I had to find some kind of sustenance.

I glanced at the floor and saw the trap door that led to the cellar. I didn't hesitate. I found the candle I'd used to light my way earlier, but it was useless without matches. I would have to make my way down and through the cellar in total darkness. I moved slowly, stealthily, knowing that the slightest noise would bring Martin down to investigate.

I paused at the bottom of the stairs that led up to the kitchen. From above I heard muffled voices. I crept up the stairs carefully, my legs throbbing from fatigue, and seated myself on the top landing, leaning close to the door to listen. The first thing I heard was Leland's voice.

'I'd like you to drive me into the university, Martin,' he said.

Obviously the hospital still hadn't checked and found me gone. Leland was going to the university, not to the hospital. He was more than likely going to lay the groundwork to explain Justin's mysterious and sudden disappearance.

'Mrs. Braddock will want to go to see her daughter later this morning, Hattie,' Leland said. 'Tell her I'll be back in plenty of time to go with her. We'd better get started, Martin, before this wind gets any stronger. If it gets worse, Hattie, tell my wife I'll stay on the mainland until it lets up.'

Footsteps moved across the kitchen and out the back entrance. I stayed huddled there on the landing, waiting until I heard the distant sound of the speedboat starting up. I glanced at the doorknob. Hattie was alone. I could hear her moving about, rattling dishes and silverware. Could I possibly chance trusting her with knowledge of my presence?

My decision was interrupted by the ringing of the telephone. I knew who was calling. It would be the hospital informing them of my disappearance. I had to think fast. Leland and Martin were out of the house. Perhaps I could confront Diana and try and reason with her.

No, I told myself, shaking my head slowly from side to side, that would be to no avail. I knew how Diana felt about Sarah. Her loyalty to Leland was too strong. She'd never help me. She was intent upon holding on to the last opportunity she had for happiness. She was old and Leland represented the only chance she had at living out her life in love and contentment. For all of Diana's maturity, her selfishness had never dimmed.

Deep inside the house I heard Hattie's high shrill voice calling Diana. I'd been right. It had been the doctor. They'd found me missing.

Hattie would be hurrying up to Diana's room. The kitchen was unoccupied. Now was my chance to try and satisfy my hunger.

I hurriedly opened the kitchen door and began snatching up pieces of bread, rolls, cold meats, fresh fruit. I found a paper sack in one of the drawers and emptied my provisions into it. Quickly I went to the refrigerator and began rummaging around for anything that caught my notice. Rather than go back into the damp, cold cellar I decided to go up the back stairs toward the solarium. I could hide myself in one of the many rooms until it was time to make our escape.

I heard footsteps. Hattie, coming back, I supposed.

I snatched up my meager bag of provisions and went toward the door to the back stairway. I pulled it open. Instantly I gasped and almost fell backward. My hands went to my mouth. My bag of provisions scattered down onto the floor. Standing on the stairs, coming slowly down into the kitchen was my mother, Diana. Hattie was directly behind her.

Diana looked as shocked and surprised at seeing me as I was at seeing her.

'Alice. You gave me a fright. What on earth are you doing here?'

I backed into the kitchen, unable to speak for a moment. Diana glanced at the clutter of food on the floor.

'What on earth are you up to, child?' she demanded.

Before I could answer, she said, 'Hattie, clean this up and bring a breakfast tray into the drawing room. I'll just have coffee but make something hot for Miss Alice. She looks famished.'

I didn't know what to do or what to say, but Diana never lost her composure. If I had indeed startled her she did not show it now. It was as though she had merely found me prowling around where I was not supposed to prowl. She eyed me from head to foot.

'You look a positive fright, my dear. Come along. Martin has a fire built in the drawing room.'

She didn't ask how I'd gotten here, but of course Diana Hamilton would never discuss anything of a personal nature before a domestic.

I followed doggedly along behind her as she went toward the drawing room. She settled herself on one of the divans flanking the blazing fire. I sat on the other divan directly across from her.

'Now what is all this nonsense about your running away from the hospital?' She was eyeing me coldly.

'You won't get away with it, Mother. Not this time.'

She gave me a blank look. 'Won't get away with what, dear? What are you talking about?'

'Stop it, Mother,' I all but shouted. 'You know I know about Sarah. I heard you and the doctor planning on having me put away — and I know why. You don't want anyone to think me sane; you want everyone to think I'm crazy, that I imagine things, just so you and Leland can go on keeping that poor girl a prisoner in this terrible old house.'

Although she retained her exterior composure, there was the slightest glimmer of weakness behind her eyes.

'Alice,' she said sharply. 'Control yourself.'

But I couldn't control myself. I suddenly broke down in a spasm of tears. I threw myself down on the sofa and cried.

Diana got up and came to me. She seated herself on the edge of the divan and began smoothing my hair. 'Hush, Alice. Hush, dear. Please don't cry, my darling. No one means you any harm. Believe me.'

'Oh, how can you say that,' I sobbed. 'I heard you and Leland plotting to put me under a psychiatrist's care. I'm not insane. You both know that.'

'Of course we know that,' she cooed. 'I really didn't mean to go through with it, dear. Honestly I didn't. I was only doing it for . . . ' She didn't finish.

I sat up quickly. I saw my opportunity for attack and I had to take it. 'For whom, Mother? For Leland? Does he mean so much to you that you'd sacrifice your own daughter? Haven't you made me suffer enough?'

'Please, Alice. Try to understand.'

'Understand? Understand what?' I was verging on hysteria and I knew it.

Hattie tapped on the door and came in carrying a breakfast tray. The momentary interruption gave me a chance to collect myself somewhat.

Hattie began pouring the coffee. 'I'll do that, Hattie,' Diana said. 'You may go. And close the doors please.'

We both sat silently as Hattie went quickly from the room, closing the doors after her.

Diana calmly poured two cups of coffee and handed me one of them. I had to admire her placidity, her complete sense of self-control. Her years as an actress had instilled that in her; whatever turbulence she felt deep inside must never show outwardly. I suddenly wished I could be like her.

'I never agreed on having you put away, Alice. Leland doesn't want that either.'

'I heard you,' I said angrily.

'You heard no such thing. You possibly heard us discussing psychiatric treatment with the doctor, but it was only talk, nothing more.'

'I don't believe you,' I said.

'That's your prerogative,' she said with a shrug of her shoulders. 'However, it is the truth.'

I put down my coffee cup and leveled a haughty gaze at her. 'You have no other choice but to have me put away,' I said. Purposely I picked up a piece of toast and began buttering it. My hand was shaking. I rested it against my knee so that it would not be noticed.

'Why do you say that?'

'Because of Sarah,' I said.

'I do wish you wouldn't continue referring to that fictional personality.'

I met her eyes. 'You know perfectly well that Sarah is not a figment of my imagination. Justin and I spoke of her. I know all about Sarah Braddock,' I said.

Diana sat forward. Her back went stiff. 'Justin told you about Sarah?'

I nodded gravely.

'Then why on earth are you insisting upon sending that poor unfortunate child to her death?'

She startled me for a moment. 'Her death?'

My trick worked, but in reverse.

Diana breathed out. Her eyes went cold again. 'Then you really don't know the truth about Sarah,' she said.

I stabbed back. 'If you mean that ridiculous story that Justin invented about Sarah being some kind of carnivorous plant . . .'

Diana's eyes widened. 'Then he did tell you,' she gasped.

'Oh, really, Mother. You can't expect me to believe such an outlandish story, that it's because she can sap life out living things.'

'It's true, Alice. It's true.'

'Well, at least you've admitted that Sarah does exist, that I didn't invent her,' I said, feeling I'd scored a victory of sorts, as empty as that victory might be.

'Yes, all right, Alice. You've tricked me into admitting it. Yes, you're right. Sarah does exist. You found her. We all know that. But you must not tell the world about her. She's ill. She's not a normal girl. She's a — a — a monster.'

'Nonsense,' I said. 'I've talked to the girl. She's as normal as you or I.' I hesitated. 'And how are you and Leland planning on explaining Justin's death?'

'Justin is not dead,' she insisted vehemently.

'I saw him. I found his body.'

'But he is not dead, Alice. He was merely unconscious when you stumbled across him.'

I hesitated. 'Did Leland tell you that? Did Leland tell you that Justin was not dead?'

'Leland would have no reason to lie to me.'

'Oh, Mother, for goodness sake, open your eyes. You're being used.'

'Alice, you don't know what you're talking about,' she said sharply, getting to her feet. She started to pace the floor. 'I love Leland,' she said softly but with immense pride.

'Oh, Mother,' I said, rushing to her and putting my arms about her. 'Please don't shut me out. I only want to help you. I want you to see what you've gotten yourself mixed up in. Shutting that girl up in that solarium is a crime. You could go to prison for it. Can't you see that?'

'That girl is dangerous. She's a monster,' Diana said.

'That's what Justin said, isn't it?' I asked anxiously trying to find some clue to the mystery surrounding Sarah.

'Yes, and he is trying to find a cure for her illness.'

'A cure? Is that why Leland killed him?'

She stared at me. 'I've told you over and over again — Justin is not dead. And please don't talk like a madwoman; Leland couldn't kill anyone, especially his own brother.'

'Sarah told me that Justin was trying to give her something to drink, some kind of medicine, she said. But Leland happened to come along and made Justin sample whatever it was he was trying to make Sarah drink.'

'Alice, be sensible. You're talking slanderously. Justin is *not* dead, I tell you. Look,' she said, glancing at the clock against the wall. 'It's almost eight. There should be people around the university who can substantiate the fact that Justin is there right now. Go ahead and call them. Go ahead.'

'I know that Leland went to the university this morning,' I told her. 'I was hiding in the cellar when he and Martin left. He most likely went to cover up his brother's disappearance.'

'If you won't believe anyone else, Alice, then please, please believe me. I *saw* Justin leave here yesterday morning. I talked with him before he left.'

It was obvious that we'd reached a stalemate; neither of us was about to give in to the other. Then Diana's shoulders sagged again. She let out a deep sigh.

'You are so very much like me, my child,' she said with a faint smile at her mouth. 'Just as obstinate and headstrong. Like you, nobody could ever make me believe them when I was your age. It's my blood that flows through your veins.' She put her arms about me. I found myself leaning against her, anxious for her embrace. 'We've hurt each other terribly, Alice. I don't know what the outcome will be, but I mean you no harm, believe that. Now I would like you to do me a favor. Let me talk with Leland when he returns.'

'No. He'll call the hospital and have them come for me.'

She patted my hand. There was a mist in her eyes. They were soft and sad. She wasn't acting now; I could tell that by merely looking at her expression.

'I don't want to lose Leland,' she said. 'But if it comes to my having to choose between you and him . . . ' she tightened her arms about me, 'I think I'll stick by my own flesh and blood. I've done you enough of an injustice, darling. I'll see that nothing happens to you again.'

She reached down and tilted my face

up to hers. Her lips brushed mine ever so lightly, ever so lovingly. 'That's a solemn promise, darling,' she said. 'Believe me.'

I honestly believed her.

18

It took me a moment or two to realize where I was when I opened my eyes. I looked toward the windows and saw them backed by the blackness of the night outside. I was in my tiny room. I'd slept away the day.

I felt refreshed and more alive than I'd felt in days. And I knew why. Diana had pampered me, fed me, fussed with my bath, brushed my hair. She wanted me with her, and the fact that she wanted me, needed me, made all the empty years without her worthwhile. She was going to appeal to Leland's sense of honor concerning Sarah. I had someone on my side at last, I thought. I was certain Diana had been sincere.

I dressed hurriedly, anxious to talk with Diana about what Leland had said about Sarah. But they weren't in their room across the hall when I went to check. I found them in the downstairs drawing room. They were arguing when I stepped off the elevator and started toward the doorway.

I hesitated. I didn't mean to eavesdrop, but they were speaking so loudly it was difficult not to.

'You're mad to have let her trick you into admitting Sarah is in this house,' Leland said.

'She knows, Leland. She's talked to the girl. There isn't any use in our pretending we can just have Alice put away like some lunatic. I couldn't bring myself to do that.'

'No one is asking that you do that,' he said. 'I thought we had agreed that we'd let the local people think what they wished about Alice. We'll send her back to California. She's only too anxious to get away from here as it is.'

'But you don't know my daughter,' Diana argued. 'If she is anything like me she will never stay silent. Oh, don't you see, Leland. We can't go on like this. Something must be done about Sarah. The mere thought that she exists in this house is driving us both to distraction.'

I edged closer to the doorway, intending to make my presence known.

'You know perfectly well that there is nothing that can be done about the child. You know what she is.'

'No, Leland, I truthfully do *not* know what she is. I only know what you've told me she is.'

He must have turned on her. He didn't speak for a second or two.

'Diana,' he breathed, 'What in God's name do you expect — a demonstration of her horrible power?' He paused. 'You don't think I hunt in the night just for the fun of it, do you?'

A short silence followed.

'I don't know what to think any more,' she said finally. Then, 'No, I suppose not, darling.'

She was weakening. I clenched my fists. I wondered if I should show myself. Perhaps if I went to Diana's side we could, between us, convince Leland to release Sarah, to tell us the real truth about her imprisonment.

'Diana,' Leland said softly. 'We cannot expose anyone to Sarah. She's capable of

just about anything. She'll destroy every-
one and anyone she chooses to destroy.
She's become an uncontrollable monster.
She almost destroyed Alice, you know.'

I stiffened.

'Alice?' Diana said with alarm.

'I didn't want to alarm you, but Justin
told me he found Alice unconscious in
Sarah's room. Alice had gone to help
Sarah escape and Sarah, for reasons of
her own, used her power on Alice. She
was sapping the strength out of her when
Justin came to her rescue.'

'Oh, no,' Diana breathed.

'Yes, Diana. It's true. Justin wouldn't
lie.'

But it wasn't Sarah, I wanted to yell
out. It was the sleeping potion that was
put in my milk. Diana had again been
swayed over to Leland's way of thinking.
How could she be so gullible as to believe
Leland's lies?

And he was lying; I was convinced of
that. Justin couldn't have told him. Justin
had promised me he wouldn't . . . and
Justin was dead. Leland had obviously
convinced Diana that Justin was still alive

and working at the university.

Well, I was back on my own again. It was up to me to get Sarah out of Falcon House. I'd do it now, this moment, if I had to carry her bodily down to the boat.

Diana started to say something else. I hesitated again.

'Can't we try and convince Alice to keep quiet about Sarah? As long as she knows the truth, surely she won't persist in trying to make trouble.'

'I can't see how we can convince her, Diana. Alice is headstrong and determined. No amount of convincing will make her see things our way. Our only hope for Sarah is to get Alice away from here — somewhere where she won't be believed when she tells her story.'

So they were again thinking of having me put away. And Diana wasn't arguing now, I noticed.

I grimaced. Where were all of Diana's pretty words to me now? Where was the sweet talk, the promises, the love she claimed she held for me? I'd been foolish to trust her, to believe her. She'd played me for a fool again and I let her do it. I had played right into her hands. She was concerned only with herself. She didn't care about me.

At least I knew where I stood. I went quickly back toward the elevator. I'd act now, and I'd act alone. I did not need Diana's help. I'd never had it before and I didn't need it or want it now. I'd get Sarah out of Falcon House forever and let the rest of them take the consequences. If I brought unhappiness down on their heads, well, that just couldn't be helped.

Angrily I jabbed the elevator button for the second level.

The upstairs hall was dimly lighted when I stepped from the elevator. I was more determined than ever that this night would be the last night Sarah would have to remain locked in Falcon House.

I tried not to make a sound as I crossed the gallery, keeping a wary eye on the entrance hall below. Again I moved through the double doors leading to the south wing, knowing that this would be the last time I'd have to take this route. Once out of Falcon House I never wanted to see or hear of it again. Sarah and I would get along well enough; the authorities would see to that.

I heard a faint scratching, clinking sound as I neared the solarium. I stopped and cocked my ear toward the sound. I wondered if Martin might possibly be in there. Cautiously I inched open the door. The glimmering wall of glass bricks met my gaze. The place was unoccupied. The scratching, clinking sound came from the other side of the glass bricks — Sarah's side — the solarium itself. It was coming from the door. She was trying to pick the lock.

I hurried over to the door and pressed myself against it.

'Sarah,' I said softly.

The clinking stopped.

'It's Alice. Can you get the door open? We've got to get away immediately.'

'Alice.' I thought I heard her chuckle low in her throat. 'Yes, I can get it open. It will only take a moment.'

She went back to her clicking and scraping and scratching with whatever she was using to open the lock. I heard a snap.

'There,' she said from the other side of the door.

I turned the knob. Sarah was standing there smiling at me. 'Let's go,' she said. 'I'm all ready.' She reached down for a small overnight case.

'No, leave that,' I said. 'We'll have to get it later on.'

I saw her bright eyes, her happy, pleasant face, her lovely long, black hair. How could they have been so cruel to think ill of this young child? She was so simple and innocent. I tried not to think of the horrible accusations they'd made concerning her. I grabbed her hand.

'Come along. We'll have to hurry,' I said.

'Where are we going?'

'First to Sheriff Anderson's office.'

She pulled away from me. 'Sheriff Anderson? Why?'

'It's our only chance, Sarah. If we go to the Sheriff and you tell him about having to stay in this old house all these years, they'll make sure you are never sent back here again. Don't you see? That way you and I will be free to go back to my home in California. Besides, we must tell him about your Uncle Justin's death.'

'No, I can't do that. I can't go to the sheriff. He'll put me in some awful place.'

'No, I won't let them do that.'

She was backing away from me, looking frightened. All of a sudden she stopped and stood still. 'Perhaps you're right,' she said with an odd, pleased look on her face. 'I really do want to get away from this dreary old place.'

I grabbed her hand and pulled her after me.

'No, not that way,' she said when I headed in the direction of the back stairs. 'Martin will be down there. It's better if we go through the main part of the house. I've always been able to get out that way before. They never think I'll use that way.'

When we got out of the south wing and were crossing the gallery, however, Diana and Leland were standing in the doorway of the drawing room downstairs.

'No,' I said in a whisper as Sarah started toward the crazy-quilt staircase.

'They'll see us for sure. We'll have to chance the back way.'

We crept silently down the back stairs. I could hear footsteps hustling back and forth in the kitchen. Sarah and I pressed ourselves flat against the stairwell and waited.

'Take this stuff out back, Martin,' we heard Hattie say. 'I'll start setting the dining room table.'

Martin's footsteps, heavy and loud went toward the back door. We heard the door open and close. Hattie went toward the interior of the house.

'Now,' I said quickly to Sarah.

I opened the door and pulled her after me. We scurried across the kitchen toward the cellar door. I pulled it open, pushed Sarah ahead of me and closed the door again. A moment later we heard Martin come in through the back of the house. We stood there in the darkness for a moment, both of us breathing heavily.

I eased by her and started to make my way slowly down the dark cellar stairs. I moved very slowly, so that my plaster cast wouldn't thump on the wooden steps and betray our presence. Sarah followed along behind me.

The cellar was blacker than I'd remembered. It was like walking through an ocean of ink. The air was thick with dampness and mildew.

'I'm getting cold,' Sarah said as she hugged herself closer to me.

'Hush. Don't talk. They might hear us.'

'I've never run away at night before. It's so cold,' she repeated in a frightened little voice.

I put an arm about her waist and led her in the direction of the vaulted passage. 'It isn't far now,' I said. 'We'll be up into the greenhouse in a couple of minutes. Hurry. This way.' Again I groped for her hand and tightened it in mine. We hurried on toward the stairway and the trap door that would take us up into the greenhouse.

Thankfully the greenhouse was lighted and unoccupied when we eased the trap door up and climbed through.

'Ah, that's better,' Sarah said, filling her lungs with the hot, humid air of the glass house. The place, to me, smelled like mold and stagnant swamp water.

'How can you appreciate this sticky old place,' I said. 'The air is so close in here.'

'I like it,' she said simply. 'Can we stay here until tomorrow when it's warm and sunny outside?'

I frowned at her. 'Of course not,' I said hastily. 'We must get away immediately. As soon as they find you missing from the solarium you know they'll start searching every inch of this island.'

'Yes, I suppose you're right,' she said indifferently. 'And they always look here first. They know I like it here.'

'You like it here?' I asked in a disbelieving tone. 'Why? This place gives me the willies.'

She strolled idly around the bins of strange, exotic flowers. 'It's all so pretty, these nice, lovely blossoms,' she said.

'Don't touch those,' I warned as I saw her reach for one of the Venus fly traps.

She held her finger toward the plant and pulled it back just as the leaves snapped closed, like a steel trap. Sarah giggled. 'I like to tease it,' she said. She put out her finger again and the leaves opened. 'It's such a silly thing; you can always fool it.'

Something down inside me started to shudder a warning. Sarah wasn't the same girl somehow. The expression on her face was more aged, more experienced. Her eyes had a harder look about them. Even when she smiled, it wasn't the innocent young girl smile I'd remembered, it was a cruel smile.

'Don't Sarah. You're making me nervous. Come along. We've got to get to the boat.'

'Oh, there's plenty of time for that,' she said.

'But there isn't plenty of time,' I argued. 'If we don't get away now we won't have another chance.'

'There will always be another chance,' she said.

She was beginning to unnerve me. 'Come on, Sarah,' I said, tugging at her arm. 'We must leave.'

'No.'

I whirled around and found her glowering at me. There was a cold, deadly look of defiance on her face. 'Sarah, what is it?' I could feel my insides begin to tremble. The expression on her face was frightening.

'You aren't going anywhere. I don't need you to help me.' She started toward me.

'Sarah,' I breathed, backing away from her.

'There is only one reason I need you.' Her smile was wicked.

'Sarah, don't play games with me,' I said. My voice was suddenly unsteady.

'I'm not playing games, pretty Alice.' She took another step forward. I took several steps away from her. I hated the way she was looking at me.

'You were stupid not to believe them,' Sarah said.

'Believe who? What are you talking about?' I bumped back against a bin of plants. Over my shoulder I saw that it was the plant bed that contained the lovely but horrible Drosera flowers. My body went stiff when I felt the touch of a leaf brush the side of my hand. I pulled my hands around me and stood there trembling as Sarah came closer and closer.

'They told you I was dangerous, didn't they?'

'Who? What? Oh, Sarah. Talk sense. Please. We must get out of here. Stop trying to frighten me.'

'But I told you. You aren't going anywhere, pretty Alice. I only wanted you to come for me so that I could be as beautiful as you.'

'Sarah, for God's sake, what are you talking about?'

'I'm talking about you, Alice. You're so beautiful. Too beautiful.' When she got within an arm's length of me she stopped. She extended her hand. I leaned away from her touch. There was something so frightening about her that I couldn't bear to look at her, yet for some reason I found it impossible to look away. Her eyes held me like a magnet.

She pointed to the Drosera flowers directly behind me. 'They are lovely, aren't they?' she said, almost as though she were in a trance. 'Almost as lovely as you. I will be lovely too,' she said.

I clutched my throat. Things Justin had

said were slowly beginning to come back to me.

'I was born there,' Sarah said. Her voice was so strange. She continued to stare at the Drosera plants. 'That is my mother.' She stepped closer. I leaned backward, but she did not come directly toward me. She stepped alongside me and stared down at the Droseras.

'I love to come and visit my mother,' she said, speaking to the bed of plants. Then she turned her head slowly toward me. 'It is difficult to say which of you is the lovelier.'

I couldn't speak. My voice was frozen with fear. Everything was becoming clear. All Justin had told me was true. They'd tried to warn me. I wouldn't believe them. Leland, Diana, even Martin tried to warn me but I wouldn't listen to any of them.

Sarah was a monster, who lived by sapping the life from others.

It hadn't been the milk that had made me lose consciousness; it had been Sarah. She had tried to take my life away and Justin had saved me. Panic gripped me. If everything they had told me about Sarah was the truth, then she meant to take my life. I had to get away from her somehow.

Sarah put her hand on my shoulder and laughed softly. 'So you are beginning to understand me, pretty Alice,' she said. 'But do not be afraid, lovely one. I'm not ready to steal your beauty away from you as yet.'

She gave a little shrug and turned back to the Drosera plants. 'Later, perhaps. When I'm in the mood.' She laughed again.

She looked down at the carnivorous plants. I stared at her, inching away from the plant bed. She suddenly reached out and grabbed my wrist and pulled me close to her. A scream caught in my throat. I was so stiff with fright that no sound came out.

'Look at them, Alice. You are as lovely as they.' She turned down her mouth. 'I was never beautiful like you, but I will be . . . now that I have you.'

'Sarah,' I breathed, finding my voice. 'We must get out of here.' I tried not to let her know just how frightened of her I actually was.

'Out of here? I can't get out of here, Alice. You should know that. I need the warmth, the humidity. I can't go out in the cold night air. I'll wither, just like my lovely Droseras would wither.' She turned her eyes on me again. I tried to cringe away. 'But, of course, you know that now, don't you, pretty Alice?'

'You're not like they say,' I argued. 'They only told you that to keep you in that solarium.' I was desperate. I felt I had to snatch at any straw within my grasp. 'The night air won't harm you.'

'Don't try to fool me, pretty Alice. You're no match for me. I know what I am and I know how I am.' Again she gave a delighted little chuckle. 'And I like being the way I am. I'm different. I'm powerful. Everyone is afraid of me. I can get anything I want once I'm away from this place. And anybody I want,' she added with another fiendish laugh.

'No, Sarah,' I moaned. 'You mustn't do this. Justin said he can cure you. Let him try. Please. We should go back.'

'Go back?' Her face was suddenly dark with rage. 'Never.'

'But if Justin can cure you, you'll be so much happier.'

'Happier? I'm happy now. I'm better than anyone else. I have powers no one ever dreamed of before. They can't cure me . . . I won't let anybody cure me.'

'But you're sick, Sarah. Don't you know that? Sick.'

She turned on me like an angered tigress. 'Sick, am I?' she shouted. She grabbed my shoulders and began shaking me. She had the strength of twenty men. I felt like a thin, fragile twig ready to be snapped in two at any moment. She shook me harder. 'I'll show you how sick I am.'

Her arms went around me. Her eyes were ablaze like those of a madwoman's. 'You think you are so much better than I,' she hissed. 'You don't think my mother is beautiful. You think you are more beautiful than she. Well we will see, my pretty Alice. We will see just who is the prettiest.'

I started to struggle as her grip

tightened on me. She was holding me so close.

'Perhaps you would like to see my mother up close,' she said. 'Perhaps you would like to find out just what her world is like. I came from there, pretty Alice. I came from that lovely place, though I was never made as beautiful as you. But I will be beautiful. I will take your beauty away from you. But first you must visit my home.'

I screamed.

I felt myself being lifted bodily up from the floor. She was raising me up, moving me toward the bed of Drosera flowers. The heavy cast on my leg seemed no burden to her. She lifted me easily, effortlessly.

I screamed again. The scream shattered the stillness of the damp, humid room. The glass panes seemed to pulse and vibrate as my scream echoed throughout the greenhouse.

Sarah lifted me high into the air and pitched me forward, into the bed of Drosera flowers. The sticky fluids on their leaves felt stingingly hot against my skin. I struggled to get free, trying to claw my way out of their midst. The leaves clung to me like so many fine, sharp steel teeth.

Sarah leaned her weight on me, holding me against the horrible flowers. The slithering leaves started to curl around me, the sticky, slimy fingers of the plants encircling my legs, my wrists, my arms. I was being pulled down into the bed. The smell was sickeningly sweet. I screamed again, but I could barely hear my own scream as the ugly, thick leaves curled and curled over my neck and face and hands.

I heard someone call Sarah's name. I saw distant shapes, distant shadows moving, fighting, spinning around in front of me. I saw Sarah's dark swirling hair move and dance in a smoky mist. I heard words, loud and angry. People moved, yelled, struggled, as I struggled.

The leaves had almost covered me completely. I felt weak, so weak that I could barely move my head. My struggles were growing fainter. The leaves were touching my cheek, crawling slowly, slowly, slowly over my mouth, covering my eyes. My hair was pulled back down into the very roots of the flowers.

Everything suddenly went black. I felt myself relaxing, falling, falling, falling down into the midst of the Droseras . . . the lovely, sweet, comfortable Drosera flowers.

I felt at peace.

19

The change was so welcome that I could only lie there and blink in the blinding kaleidoscope of color, dazed by the brilliant oranges and yellows and vivid colors that swam before my eyes.

'Alice,' Diana said softly, touching my brow with her lips.

I smiled up at her. 'I seem to be a terrible burden to you,' I said. My voice was so soft and so delicate that I almost did not hear it myself.

'Everything will be all right now.'

I suddenly remembered the horrible nightmare of being thrown bodily into the Drosera flowers. I sat up, scanning the lovely drawing room with its beautiful colors, its bright, cozy fireplace, its comfortable furniture.

'There, there, child,' Leland said, easing me back against the cushions. 'You've had a frightful experience. Rest, dear. As your mother said, everything will be all right now.'

'But Sarah?' I asked in an anxious, worried voice.

'Unfortunately she ran away from us. Martin is out searching. He'll find her. She can't have gone very far.'

I glanced toward the window. Daylight was streaming in through the delicate lace curtains. 'It's morning.'

'Afternoon,' Diana corrected with a smile. 'You have been unconscious for quite awhile, darling. Are you hungry?'

I shook my head. 'No, not really, Mother. It's just . . . ' Suddenly tears flooded my eyes and ran down my cheeks. I started to sob.

Diana enfolded me in her arms. 'Don't cry, darling. Everything will work out for the best now.'

'But Sarah may perish if she's been out in the night all this time,' I said through my tears.

'Don't fret about Sarah,' Leland put in. 'I was very foolish to think I could keep her a secret forever. Perhaps you have done us a great favor, Alice, by forcing us to face the facts. The child is dangerous, as you know by now. Perhaps it would be a godsend if the cold night air did take her and put her to rest.' There were tears in his eyes.

Hattie suddenly came bustling in with something steaming hot in a bowl. 'I've brought you some broth, Miss Alice. Try and drink some now and get your strength back.'

Diana took the broth from her and began spooning it, bit by bit, into my mouth. The heat of the broth began to put warmth back into my limbs, yet it tasted odd. After several spoonfuls I pushed it away. 'I'm really not at all hungry,' I told Diana.

'Very well, dear,' she said. She handed the broth back to Hattie. 'Hattie will keep it warm in case you want a little more later on.'

I sat up. My head felt so light, so strange. Everything seemed so much clearer somehow. Diana looked more beautiful, Leland more handsome. Even the atmosphere of the house — not just the drawing room but the entire house — seemed lovely, more comfortable. I told myself that it was because the mystery of Sarah Braddock was solved. There wasn't anything hidden from me now. Diana and Leland were not really the monsters I'd believed them to be.

'Justin.' I said the name without realizing I'd said it.

'Justin and I spoke on the telephone. He said he'd be coming over sometime today to show you he is still flesh and blood,' Leland said. 'He's been working on a new potion for Sarah.'

I looked up at Leland. The tears were still seeping from my eyes. 'Oh, Leland. I'm so ashamed of myself for all the terrible things I thought and said and did.'

'Now, there is no need for apologies. You did and said what you thought was right. I admire you for it. If anyone is due an apology, it is you. We should have told you the truth about Sarah right at the start.'

'But Justin did tell me. I wouldn't believe him,' I said.

'Well, I suppose I can't blame you for

that,' Leland said. 'It is rather a fantastic story.'

I frowned up at him. My mind started to think over my encounter with Sarah in the greenhouse. 'Leland?' I started. 'When Sarah and I were in the greenhouse, she kept referring to the Drosera flowers as her mother. What did she mean?'

He gave a wry little smile but his eyes were deadly dark. 'Well,' he said, 'when Sarah was only a wee tot her mother died. Sarah wandered into the greenhouse — she'd always been attracted to flowers . . . '

'Yes,' I interrupted, cutting him off. 'Justin told me about her drinking a formula you used for feeding the Droseras.'

He nodded. 'But that wasn't the end of it.' He sighed. 'Sarah was a sick little girl for a long time. When she recovered she was constantly running away to the greenhouse and crawling up into the Drosera flowers. Strangely enough they would hug her tightly but never smother her as they tried to do to you, which is their usual nature.

'Of course, the Drosera plants I cultivate here are a very special variety. The usual Drosera flowers would offer no bodily harm to a human. These that I have cultivated, unfortunately have been developed to a very high state. They could easily have devoured you completely if Martin and I hadn't pulled you out of them in time. As it was, I am surprised that you suffered no ill effects from your ordeal. They are an extremely poisonous growth.'

He picked up my hand and began to examine my arm closely. 'Usually the sting of the liquid on the leaves penetrates the skin. It can cause death.' He continued to scrutinize my arm. 'Oddly enough the leaves did you no harm . . . no harm at all. That's extremely odd.'

I shuddered and pulled back my hand. 'Thank heaven you heard me scream,' I said.

'We'd found you and Sarah gone. The greenhouse is always the first place she heads for. It was just unfortunate that we didn't reach you earlier.'

'But I still don't understand why she thinks the flowers are her mother.'

Leland gave a helpless little gesture by fanning out his hands. 'Who knows what kind of ideas the child conjured up in her little head when she was unconscious after drinking the formula? She never had a mother. I suppose the formula in some way linked her to the flowers . . . she felt a kinship there. She was always mortally afraid of me for some unknown reason. Naturally I've never harmed the girl in my entire life, but she feared me terribly. She wanted a mother in the worst way. She obviously adopted the Drosera plants.'

'When I first found Sarah,' I said, 'she told me that you'd been disgraced in some way in your work.'

Leland nodded gravely. 'That is very true. I was laughed out of the Institute for introducing a theory I had wherein the aging process of humans could be interrupted by an injection of a certain fluid which I extracted from several different species of carnivorous plants. It's true, but they said I was a lunatic. I became a laughing stock, so I retired here to Falcon Island and wanted nothing more to do with that world out there until I could show them proof of my theory.'

'And do you have such proof?'

He gave me a pleased little look. He cocked his head to one side and put a lopsided smile on his lips. 'How old would you say Sarah is?'

I shrugged. 'My age, perhaps a few years younger.'

'She's older than Justin, and he's thirty-six. Sarah is forty-eight years old.'

'Forty-eight,' I breathed. 'Why that's incredible. She looks in her teens.'

'Precisely,' he said. 'When Sarah accidentally drank the formula, it slowed down her aging process. This is what led me to the discovery of my theory. I've proven the theory with animals of all sorts. I have never had the courage to experiment on another human being. I'm not that positive that the formula is right as yet.

'And of course I can't produce Sarah as evidence because she must always be kept in a damp, humid climate. Anyway, no one would believe me about Sarah because when we first realized her power of taking life from the living, we had to invent some excuse for hiding her away. I released a news announcement that Sarah died. A doctor who knew the truth about Sarah, the doctor who treated her during her sickness, signed the death certificate and we held a mock funeral.

'It was all very grotesque, but necessary. She'd killed several people. I couldn't bring myself to turn her over to the police because they certainly wouldn't believe my story and Sarah would just go on killing whoever she chose. I felt my hands were tied, so Justin and I decided to keep her presence in Falcon House a deep secret.'

He glanced at Diana, reached out and took her hand. 'But then, I fell in love,' he said. 'I've never been so much in love. Oh, I tried marriage once after Sarah's mother died, but that proved to be a dreadful mistake.'

'Yes,' I said, nodding. 'Sheriff Anderson mentioned it to me.'

He patted Diana's hand. 'When Justin

introduced me to Diana I made a vow to do something I'd never done before — try to take something away from my younger brother,' he said, laughing. 'I really didn't think I had a chance, but Justin was always a kind of wild, unsettled type. I often wonder if he'll ever marry at all. So, I went after Diana and I won her.'

'No,' Diana said, pressing her hand in his. 'I won you, my darling.'

They stood there looking lovingly into each other's eyes. My own eyes grew misty.

'I told Diana about Sarah before we married. She, like you, didn't really believe my story. You two are very much alike, you know.'

'Of course,' Diana said brightly. 'Why shouldn't we be? She is my only flesh and blood.' She beamed at me. 'And I am very proud of her.'

Leland patted her hand again. 'Actually, I don't really think Diana believed my story about Sarah until tonight.'

'That isn't altogether true. Leland,' Diana said. 'I knew you would never lie to me about anything.'

'Still in all,' Leland said. 'You used to become very annoyed with me for dragging you around in the middle of the night to hunt in the forest.'

'Doesn't that prove that I believed you,' Diana said. 'You don't know your wife very well,' she added, laughing. 'I would not let any man drag me around in a dark, wet forest if I didn't totally and completely love and believe in him.'

There was a slight hesitation in the conversation.

I looked up at Leland and said, 'And you think Justin can produce a cure for Sarah?'

He shrugged his shoulders. 'Justin thinks he can. I'm not so sure. I'm so afraid an unproven remedy might prove harmful. I don't want him to chance it without extensive research.'

'Is that what happened when I found Justin unconscious in Sarah's room? Was Justin trying to force her to drink an unproven medicine?'

Leland looked uncomfortable. 'Yes,' he said shortly. Then he scanned the room, looking toward the doors. 'I wonder where Martin is? Surely he's found Sarah by this time.'

I had the odd impression that Leland was deliberately directing the conversation away from Justin. I wondered why.

'Perhaps we should go and look for him,' Diana said. 'It is almost two o'clock.'

Out of the blue, something happened to me. I can't explain exactly what, but a hot, searing wave of fire seemed to sweep through my brain. I went hot all over and then cold, very cold. I must have swayed because Diana touched my shoulder and asked, 'Are you all right, Alice?'

'Yes, I think so,' I said, rubbing my temples. 'I felt so strange for a second or two. I can't understand it.'

'The Drosera poison may have gotten into your system without our realizing it,' Leland put in. 'I'll arrange for you to have a complete physical examination tomorrow.'

'No, no,' I said quickly. 'I'm all right. Really I am. Whatever it was is gone now. I feel fine.'

'No matter,' Leland persisted. 'I think a

complete physical would do you no harm.'

'No!' I actually shouted it at him. My voice was so loud, so harsh that I surprised even myself. Leland and Diana were looking at me with disbelief. 'I'm sorry,' I muttered, rubbing my temples again. 'I'm tired, that's all.' I saw Diana and Leland exchange strange, knowing looks.

I glanced toward the windows. The sun was shining brightly. It looked like such a very hot day outside, and yet I felt chilled to the bone. I noticed that the fireplace was blazing away. Its warmth looked so attractive, so magnetic, yet it seemed odd to have a fire blazing on such a seemingly warm, pleasant day. I got up slowly and went toward the fire, holding out my hands to it. The heat felt magnificent.

When I happened to turn around abruptly, I noticed that Diana and Leland were again looking at each other strangely.

'The fire feels so good,' I said, wrapping my arms around myself. 'Strange that it should be so cold in here and yet it seems so warm outside.'

'The house is tricky,' Leland said casually. 'There are so many, many drafts everywhere. We built the fire thinking that you might need it when you gained consciousness.'

'Why?'

He shrugged and didn't answer. He turned away from me.

I thought Diana looked overly warm and slightly flushed. I felt so cold, so very, very cold. Leland too had a strange, overheated look about him. He was dressed only in shirt sleeves. I noticed wet areas of perspiration at the arms.

'If you're feeling stronger, darling, I think perhaps Leland and I should go off and search out Martin. He's prowling the island for Sarah. She had a number of favorite places where she likes to hole up when she gets out of the solarium,' she said.

'Of course, Mother,' I said brightly. 'I'm feeling much, much better now. I'll stay here for a while, then perhaps I'll lie down in my room. I still feel a bit weak.'

Why had I said that? I wondered. I didn't feel weak at all. On the contrary, I felt very strong, stronger than I ever felt in my entire life. Even the cast on my leg felt weightless.

I couldn't understand the strange and sudden change that seemed to be moving over me. I felt a stranger unto myself. A light, carefree bubble was lifting me up, raising my spirits, making me happier than I'd ever felt before. It was as if I had never existed until this very moment. As I stood before the fireplace looking at Diana and Leland, I felt transported. I was in a completely different world where no one existed except my mother, my stepfather and the people I'd met on Falcon Island.

I suddenly never wanted to leave this lovely place. The house seemed warm and cozy. The whole atmosphere of the place was opening its arms to me, enfolding me, welcoming me home.

'Are you sure you are all right, dear?' Diana said. 'You look rather strange.'

'I'm fine,' I beamed. 'I can't understand why I feel so very good, but I do.'

'You've been through so very much since coming here,' Leland said. 'You're most likely finally relaxing now that everything is clear to you.'

'Yes,' I said. 'I suppose that's it. I never felt so alive, so lightheaded, so carefree before.'

Diana came over and put her arm about my waist. She headed me toward the door. 'I think you'd best not overtax yourself, darling. Why don't you go up to your room and lie down? I'll have Hattie fix you some more broth and a sandwich. You must be famished.'

'I am, and yet I'm not,' I said.

Again I saw Diana and Leland look strangely at each other.

'I know I should be hungry.' I gave a little laugh. 'I'm always hungry as a rule. And yet I can't explain the need I feel inside of me.'

Diana suddenly swayed, coming dangerously close to collapsing against me. 'Oh, dear,' she moaned, putting her hand to her head. 'I suddenly feel so faint.'

Leland hurried to support her. He pulled her away from me and frowned. His face was suddenly the color of death. 'I'm going to see both of you to bed,' he said sternly. 'Then I'm going out to search for Martin and Sarah. Come along, you two.'

We grouped ourselves inside the elevator and started upward. Diana was leaning heavily on Leland.

'It's so close in here,' Leland said suddenly, mopping his brow with his handkerchief. 'I can't understand it.' I noticed that he was avoiding my eyes.

The door opened on the second level. Leland helped Diana out, letting me straggle along behind them alone. They both looked oddly off balance for some reason or other. It was like the blind leading the blind. Neither of them spoke as they went toward their room. At their door Diana turned.

'Get some rest, child. We'll call you only when dinner is ready to be served. Don't stir until then. You really could use some sleep.'

'We all could,' Leland said. He looked so very nervous.

'Come along, Diana,' he said, hurrying her into their room. The door closed soundly after them.

★ ★ ★

Martin had indeed found Sarah. Leland had come to tell me that my prediction had been right. When she ran into the cold night, she'd lost all her strength. They found her lying dead at the foot of one of the palm trees.

Now it was night again. I went toward the window when I thought I heard the sound of a motorboat in the distance.

My muscles were screaming out for warmth and humidity. The room was like an ice chest. My body was shivering. I felt weak, almost to the point of expiring. I knew what had happened. When she had flung me into the Droseras, they had adopted me, as they had Sarah. I had become what she had been.

A tiny housefly butted up against the pane, trying in vain to find its way out into the open air. I watched its futile attempts. I felt so like that ill-fated fly. Unconsciously I leaned toward it. My breath stung its fluttering wings. The little insect dropped dead at my feet.

Tears started to stream out of my eyes,

down my cheeks.

I raised my eyes to the light, bright loveliness of the sky. I felt a sudden wave of peaceful serenity sweep over my body.

I saw movement down on the terrace. I gasped and stiffened when I saw Leland and Diana appear below me, Hattie and Martin following them. They were dressed and packed for travelling. They were leaving me here, alone.

No, I screamed inside my head. Diana hadn't changed. She still thought only of herself. Yet, I didn't blame her for leaving me. I wanted her to go. I had to be alone. From the very beginning I was meant to be alone.

As they stepped from the terrace Diana turned toward the windows of the solarium. She raised her eyes to mine. She pressed the fingers of her gloved hand to her lips and threw me a kiss. Even from the distance that separated us I could see the tears glimmering in her eyes and rolling down her pale, sunken cheeks.

'Goodbye, my darling,' she mouthed. I saw her lips move, the words form.

I raised my hand, knowing that this was the end. I wanted them to leave me now. I wanted to have all of them go; no one should stay. I meant only death for others.

I watched the little parade as it went toward the jetty. Then Justin came out of the house and followed the little procession down to the boat. I couldn't watch them leave. I turned away from the window and seated myself on the edge of the narrow bed. I could see Diana turning and waving with my mind's eye. The sound of the motor boat came and went, and I was alone.

The house was like a tomb. The silence was deafening. A strange gnawing started again in the pit of my stomach and I knew what I had to do. The idea was so odious that my hands clenched into fists and a wave of nausea washed over me. Yet, I couldn't help myself. I had to find nourishment. The need to survive was strong, stronger than I thought possible. I had to replenish the strength that was easing away from me. There were animals on the island. I would take their life for my own.

I made my way to the elevator. When I stepped into the entrance hall I stopped dead in my tracks. Justin Braddock was standing in the open doorway.

'Are you ready?' he said softly.

'Justin, no. Please. Go away. Go with them. Leave me. You don't know what you're doing.'

'I know only too well, my darling,' he said. He came toward me, reaching out to take my hand. I backed away from him.

'No, Justin. You mustn't. I'm like her. I'm like Sarah.'

'Yes, Leland told me,' he said, his eyes bright with happiness, his smile warm and loving.

'I don't understand,' I said, continuing to shrink away from him.

'The potion. Sarah forced it onto me. We're alike you and I, Alice. We're together. No one can ever separate us.'

'I don't believe you,' I moaned.

He stepped toward me.

'No, Justin. Please. Go away.'

He merely smiled at me. 'Try your powers on me, Alice. You will find they are useless. My powers are like yours and they cannot be used against each other. Sarah, in her own strange way, wanted it this way, I suppose. She knew when she gave me the potion that I would become like her. Knowing this, she wanted me to be happy. She threw you into the Drosera plants in a fit of rage, but subconsciously I think she wanted us to be together. I know that's what I want, Alice, dear. I have never wanted anything so much.'

I was speechless.

'You don't really think that Diana and Leland would go off and leave you entirely alone, do you? They knew about me — at least Leland suspected. When he came to the university that morning with Martin, he found me unconscious. A cage of pet rabbits had been opened in the laboratory and all their lifeless bodies were strewn about. Then, when I told him about the potion that Sarah forced down me, he knew. We both knew.'

'Oh, no, Justin,' I cried. 'No.'

'We mustn't fight it, darling. We have a life to live. We shall do it together, if that's what you wish.'

Happiness comes in strange forms. I

felt it wash over me as I rushed into Justin's arms. He hugged me close and we kissed.

'Oh, Justin,' I sighed.

'I'll never leave you, Alice.'

We stood looking lovingly into each other's eyes. Then we turned, arms about each other, and went slowly toward the forest.

THE END